Despicable People

Eric David Roman

Wholly Roman Press

1st-ish edition

ISBN 10: 0692693440
ISBN 13: 9780692693445

TO MY DESPICABLE PEOPLE

To my Husband, for loving and putting up with me, which by law he kind of has to do anyway.

To my Whores who are the best support system a guy with low morals can have.

To Bob and Kelli, thank you forever and infinity.

And to John Waters,
thank you for all the continued inspiration.

1. Desperate Living

"It is so odd to find myself in this predicament. I mean really here I am on Friday evening. The sun is setting and all of my friends are otherwise engaged, and I am just staring into the abyss. Not really knowing what to do all on my own. It's rarer than a lunar eclipse actually. Normally my weekends are filled, never a dull moment kind of thing ya know. By this time, I've left work and am heading over to Craig and Andy's for our traditional pre-dinner mojitos. That leads into the thirty-minute conversation about where or what we want to eat. A chorus of "wherever I don't care" in a tediously repetitive round robin. I mean really, someone at some point has to fucking care. No one can ever make a damn decision and we just go back and forth. When a place is finally decided we're already pretty buzzed and usually Sylvia or Claire have joined us by that time. Harold sometimes is there, but he's usually working and doesn't show up till later. He gets pissed we're all hammered and he has to play catch-up. But I tell him, I say, Harold, get the fuck out of retail and then you can come have drinks at a reasonable time like a normal person. Then dinner is finally decided and we head out. More drinks consumed while waiting for the food, then a bar after maybe or a movie. Craig usually has Saturday morning mapped out with some activity that drags us out of the city. It is usually a blur and then by Sunday evening we all retreat to our separate lives. Though we still text each other until all the Sunday evening shows are over. Why we don't just stay together until after the shows are over is beyond me.

Not this weekend though, no sir, this weekend everyone but me is caught up with family functions or work commitments. I call it the Unicorn day because it's a rare as a Unicorn to be left on my own. Though I know Unicorns aren't even real, but I like the sound of it. Albino humpback whale day doesn't have the same ring.

I mean I guess I could try to get laid, seeing how I am between insignificant others at the moment. But all I'd be doing is spending countless hours staring at my phone on whichever hook-up app I choose to use. Then begins the "tweaking" or I guess we can call it outright lying, I mean who are we kidding here? Nothing big really, plus all those other guys are lying too of course. I just don't want to be catfishing all night, it's far more work than most people know. I have to lie about my age; thirty-three becomes twenty-nine. My weight magically loses those ten extra pounds I seem to have right now being post-relationship. To clarify I dumped him.

I'm never sure if five foot eight sounds short or not. I mean on what scale are people judging this really? Like 'Tom Cruise' to 'Asian basketball player'? I'm no hobbit but I would not mind being a couple of inches taller. I have this really short friend Cecil and I swear to God people are constantly throwing rings at him and

pointing him in the direction of Mordor. In the end, I'll
have accomplished nothing but soliciting invites from
dudes I don't want to fuck and have gotten rejections
from the dudes I do want to fuck. It is just a lot of work
that eats away all the time and then if I happen to finally
narrow it down and invite someone over, the awkward
sex lasts like twenty minutes and then leads to an even
more awkward goodbye. Do I offer to let him use my
shower? Do I give him a real bath towel or throw some
paper towels at him and tell him to clean up in the
corner? If I give him the actual one, what do I do with
that semen covered towel? I don't even want to touch it.
After he finally does leave, I'd be right back where I
started, that's a lot of fucking work for a potentially
lackluster blowjob, know what I mean?"

I am met with nothing but a blank stare. Jekyll,
the lavender hair colored, mid-forties frumpish co-owner
of the Underground video store I am in just glares at me.
She sighs heavily, "Derek," she says pointedly, "what
part of my face says 'please tell me everything about
your fucking life'? No, really, because whatever it is I
need to know so I can go into the alley out back and have
a rat remove it from my face, so this," she waves her
fingers at me, "never fucking happens again."

Perhaps I overshared.

I did only approach the counter to see what is new
that might have come in. I smile embarrassedly and
wander away from the counter into the store.

Video stores are an extinct creature now, but I am
lucky to have this little gem, Jekyll and Hyde's
Underground Video, still surviving in my city. It is also
conveniently located in the block between the subway
stop and my apartment so I am more than a frequent
customer. Though judging from Jekyll's face just now, I
could be barred at any moment.

Jekyll and Hyde are a cute married couple, slightly older than I am, who somehow managed in the age of digital downloads and streaming services to keep the doors opens on this secret cinema treasure chest. They changed over from a rental store to a retail store when they sensed the shift happening. I still have my rental membership card from when I first moved into my apartment in 2003. They never followed traditional video store politics, the shelves are not organized by genres, and nothing is alphabetized. Items are everywhere, mixed together in a media orgy. The idea is while you hunt for the title you came in for, you may possibly come across a gem you did not know you even wanted to see. Thanks to this deliriously fucked up system I had found some great movies. Though I have seen weaker willed people get so frustrated they threatened to burn the place down on their way out empty-handed. Jekyll and Hyde would just laugh at them as the door slammed. Somehow they always know where everything is, and if they've seen you put up a good fight looking for a specific item they may eventually help you, but probably not.

Even now the medium-sized, below street level store was packed with every format available, VHS, BETA, laserdisc, regular DVD and of course Blu-rays. So your possibilities of coming across something new and unseen was infinite. If you were deemed worthy enough and had the right equipment they'd let you into the back to see the collection of actual films. Eight and sixteen-millimeter reels. I heard from an acquaintance I blew once at a party overrun with straight people, that they had a secret stash of actual thirty-five-millimeter films, classic and rare ones. A real find if you happened to have a projector to screen it. It was called Underground Video for a reason, no family fare, no light-hearted comedies here. The worse the better was the motto in this den of cinema depravity. It is heaven on earth.

I was indeed, as I told an unwilling to listen Jekyll, all on my own for the weekend. Though I did have a plan, a tentative plan mind you, one easily shoved aside if the chance to get some dick should happen to arise. Though I was most certainly not in the mood, I would probably just lay there and exert the least amount of energy. That's just awful. No one likes a lazy bottom. Ever since my breakup, I'd become increasingly lazy. It's not that I'm depressed over the breakup. That dude was so fucking boring. I mean, I am all for a night in watching Netflix and getting stoned, but a documentary about taking down dams and returning the river to nature? Please people were crying in joy because the salmon had come back. Not my idea of riveting excitement. *Romy and Michelle's High School Reunion* is on Netflix too ya know, so let's get our life together okay?

Sure, my latest breakup returned me to the only single one among my group of friends. Craig and Andy are married, Harold has two boyfriends, who don't know about each other, Sylvia has a really butch girlfriend who frightens me, and Claire is our token straight friend whose husband is so scared to be around gay men that he never hangs out with us. Please, like any self-respecting gay man would be pushing people out of the way to get in line to suck the obviously small cock of that bald, over-weight accountant. I adore Claire though so I just ignore him.

My love life is a total disaster. Before boring guy, there was the older guy who seemed to get turned on by car crashes. Not in a hot J.G Ballard *Crash* kind of way, but in a very disturbing real way. He was a short-lived affair thankfully. I think he died actually, but eh, who cares. If it was in a car accident than I am sure he went happy. I'm not unattractive, well at least I don't think so anyway. I have a mop of messy brown hair on my head that could use a trim. I have an adorable boyish face. Which I'm trying to cover with a sad mockery of a beard at the moment to give me that rugged Lumbersexual vibe that seems to be so popular. But alas my beard is still in its infancy and lacks any of that sexual prowess other beards seem to have.

I am about to resign myself to a future of iffy Craigslist ads. Maybe I'll open the door and after a hopefully good fuck, the maniac will kill me. Relationship issue solved. As I peruse the shelves looking for something to watch I think of what kind of funeral that would lead too. Would anyone say it was my lustful desire for a piece of strange that led to my demise? Would my tearful parents lie to everyone and say it was a robbery gone wrong? Would anyone believe them or would they look at me in the tasteful velvet-lined coffin and smirk at my corpse, calling me a "whore" under their breath?

It is why most nights I give up on the hook-up apps, smoke a bowl and go to bed. I don't need the pressure of my would-be funeral on my conscious as I try to maintain an erection with some stranger who lied about his height.

My plan for the weekend is pretty simple and lacking any and all effort. No Craig to make me go apple picking, taste testing artisanal cheeses made from various farm animals, I didn't even know produced milk. Cheeses crafted by Hippie women who haven't shaved their armpits or their legs in many, many moons. 'MMMM' I say, having to lie while eating their disgusting cheeses. All while trying to ignore their repellent body odor, which somehow even with being outside in the fresh air, is still ripe, pungent and overwhelming. Or there is the absolute worst in all of the activities – hiking. Don't you fucking hate people who hike? I do. They're always so goddamn smug like they are all superior because they got up early, strapped on some asshole couture and went traipsing through some goddamn wilderness. While I just stayed home jerking off to HGTV. And they're always going on and on about whatever mountain or trail they recently hiked, referring to it by name like I am supposed to know where they're fucking talking about. They won't be so damn smug the next time when they have to have their lost asses airlifted out. Assholes.

No, the plan involves nothing but take-out food, preferably Chinese. My stash of weed and then camping out on the couch in the darkened living room to binge-watch movies. It's not like I am the biggest pothead or anything. I don't wake and bake or do it before work or social engagements, but after a stressful day, it helps take the edge off. And on a rare weekend like this it is the perfect companion for my manic marathon of cinema.

Nothing is jumping out at me though. I look over and see Jekyll behind the counter flipping through a magazine. She shoots me the eyes and I duck my head down and return to looking.

Seen it, seen it, don't want to see it. Oh, look a copy of Peter Jackson's *Meet the Feebles*. A depraved version of the Muppets complete with STD's and songs about sodomy. In my opinion Peter's best work. Fuck Lord of the Rings, a deranged scorned female Hippo with an automatic gun on a violent bloody rampage beats homoerotic hobbits any day. I make a mental note of this title for later viewing since I already own it at home. *My evening viewing needs a theme* I think as I slink down the aisle looking at more titles.

I could do a cannibal theme, but really watching *Cannibal Holocaust* once in life is more than enough. It certainly does not ever need to be viewed in high definition. I quickly scan the rest of the titles in the section but nothing jumps out at me except Nacho Cerada's *Aftermath*. The only film I ever had to turn off. Not only did I turn it off, but I also had to leave the room, compose myself and came back a half-hour later to finish it. I am a completest. In it, a mortician becomes attracted to the body of young car crash victim but doesn't engage in the act of necrophilia until *after* he does the autopsy. Yeah, that is the kind of shit you can find when you are looking for something else. I fucking love this store.

My search is leading nowhere when it hits me. *I am out of pot*. It can't be, but the inner voice rattling around my head is telling me it is so. Sitting on my bookshelf, in my apartment is the vintage metal He-Man and the Masters of the Universe lunchbox that houses my stash. I realize it has been empty since Wednesday. I shared with the gang the weekend before and I had forgotten to call my dealer and get more before the end of the week. Dammit! This is why I keep telling my boss I need a secretary.

I have a very good relationship with Barnabas, my dealer, and good relationship or not, I do not like making those frantic calls for drugs at the last minute. I like to believe I have more composure than that. Yet my whole plan for this weekend which mainly consisted of me being stoned to the bone now hangs in the balance. I curse out loud. Mad at myself for my own forgetfulness. I pull my phone out of my pocket and resist. What can I say so I don't sound desperate? I do not need to put on airs with Barnabas but still, I'd like to feel like I have a modicum of self-respect. I bite the bullet and text him. I apologize for the last-minute nature of my request and ask if is he is available.

I return to looking through the stacks of films. Waiting anxiously for the phone to go off in my hand. I know technically it is his job, seeing how he is a drug dealer and all. But I know he also works at Whole Foods. I can't really expect him to drop the Flaxseed and Wasabi peas he's shelving. Or interrupt his conversation about all the natural benefits of Coconut Oil with some yoga pants wearing soccer mom, just to run over and help me in my time of need. It seems like forever when finally a response.

My heart stops when I read it, he tells me he is in Puerto Rico!

What about the Wasabi peas?

He apologizes and says he texted me earlier in the week seeing if I needed anything before he left.

LIES! Had he? I had been busy with work, as an office manager for a magazine it has its stressful times. It seems odd I would have missed a text from him. I scroll through my phone to see if he was telling the truth, he was. It does not matter, nothing can be done now. I respond that I missed it, totally my fault and tell him to have fun on his trip.

Fuck, what was I to do now? I'm a thirty-four-year-old white guy. It's not like I know a lot of drug dealers. Before I met Barnabas a couple of years ago, I would only sit around and talk about getting high. Drug dealers are people you know in your twenties. Once you leave college and outgrow your party phase, the drug dealers fall away naturally. The fevered flush of desperation fills my body. I'm certain the store is getting hotter, I may faint. I look around, dammit, not a fainting couch within sight. It's going to be straight to the cold hard floor if it happens.

My phone vibrates again. He thanks me for wishing him a good trip. Aww, he is a super polite guy, but I don't give a shit about his fucking trip. I am in crisis mode now and that is all that matters. Besides, I'm sure his Facebook page will be filled with pictures soon enough.

There is nothing worse than being at work or stuck at home, broke as fuck. Then you look at your Facebook feed. Some dick is filling up your newsfeed with their wonderful vacation photos. No, I don't want to see a picture of your fucking hotel room. Hotel rooms are hotel rooms. Unless you got a motherfucking rock star level suite, I and the rest of the world don't give a shit. I don't need to see a picture of the cruise ship with some assholish headline: Look how big it is! Yeah, fucker we know it's big, it's a cruise ship. I hope your captain gets drunk and sinks it into the Aegean you ignorant fuck.

Assholes.

Look, I don't want to begrudge anyone a good time, but I will, because I'm petty like that.

Another text comes through. I can feel Jekyll's beady eyes on me. Phones are forbidden in this hallowed place. I look up and smile at her; she sighs again and goes back to the Fangoria magazine she is reading. I silence my phone and read Barnabas' text. He says if I am in a real need he can hook me up with someone who can help me out. Even out of the country, well kinda, he is still a super nice guy. I almost feel bad about not caring about his vacation.

I said almost. I know the minute I scroll through my newsfeed there's going to be a picture of his meal. And then I'll really get fucking annoyed.

A stranger though? I'd have to go meet someone? A new person, is there anything worse than new people? Some perky fuck who'll want to know what music I like or worse, discuss politics. The only politics I know or care about are those pertaining to Westeros.

So, it's either go see a stranger and buy drugs or just stay home and drink all weekend. *But I like weed so much more.* I whine to myself. No hangover, no hugging a toilet puking and declaring there will be no more drinking. Plus I'm alone, I can't drink alone. I mean a bottle or two of wine sure, but past that it's socially unacceptable. As if he can almost tell my hesitation he texts me saying, his friend is cool and I shouldn't worry. Just go see him.

I agree.

What the fuck, Chinese food will still be there once this new errand is over. He sends me back a smiley face and says he checking with his friend to make sure I can swing by. All I can think now is what seedy part of this damn city am I going to have dredge into. Somewhere where the cabs don't or won't go most likely. Barnabas is one of those black guys who are very non-threating and he even sounds like a white person when he talks. But I have no idea where he gets his shit from. Maybe he goes into the ghetto once a week and becomes a whole different person while wheeling and dealing. Maybe he holds his gun sideways and pops caps in asses.

Jesus, that's racist.

He texts me again and thankfully the dude is at the college, which is closer, yeah that's it *closer*. I mean, I would have gone to the ghetto if I had too, but a delicate homosexual like myself cannot be wandering around the south side of the city looking to score drugs. Yes, the college is a better option, but still, I'm hesitant. I like drugs, I want the drugs, but I just don't want to go get the drugs. It is kinda seedy and I don't like to feel seedy. Well normally.

I check my phone and once again on cue Barnabas seems to know what I was feeling hundreds of miles away. He assures me it will be fine and that to remember his motto: 'The only way to live life is to go along with where it takes you.' Yep, there it is solid hippie wisdom from the man who brushes his teeth with coconut oil.

I grab Jodorowsky's *The Holy Mountain* since I don't own it. You can't really leave the store without buying anything or Jekyll and Hyde send you an email - a vicious, unapologetic, horridly vivid email degrading your person and having dealt with that once was enough for me. I place my purchase down on the counter and Jekyll sighs again. She rings me up and then flips me the bird instead of thanking me for my patronage. I take my movie, sans bag, let her know I'll be back and head out to run my little errand and start my lazy weekend.

2: Pecker

It was still pretty early in the evening by the time I arrived at the college campus. The sun is all but a sliver of light. Which I feel is good since I am engaging in illegal activities, and I'd prefer to do that under the cover of darkness. I don't need that judgmental bastard of a sun looking down on me.

I had gone home first naturally. It is only a block away from the video store and I wanted a snack and to change my clothes. That became a longer endeavor than I had planned, but really what does one wear to go solicit drugs from a stranger? The subject is not really covered in any etiquette books I've read. In my usual Derek way, I overthink it and go through three different outfits. One, my relaxed suit look from the office seemed far too preppy. By relaxed, I mean suit jacket, nice shirt, no tie. Fuck ties. They are assholes that spend all day trying to strangle you. I feel I look just as dapper sans the tie thank you very much. Would that outfit make me stick out like a sore thumb amongst the college kids?

Nix the suit.

Then I think I will dress more to what the college kids are wearing. I could blend in like a chameleon, sneak in, score the drugs, and then sneak out. No one would be the wiser. I am determined for a good twenty-two minutes that this was the right decision until I realize – I have no clue what the fuck they wear. I attempted the best I could and the result - a thirty-four-year-old man trying to look young and ending up looking like a sad reject from a failed CW pilot. Why can't this guy just deliver the drugs? I'd pay extra dammit.

I'm sure all kinds of people are roaming the campus, and no one gives a shit. I went to what I always go to, my favorite pair of jeans, a vintage-looking Masters of the Universe T-shirt, and my trusty thin grey and blue hoodie. Not sure if this ensemble counts as a "look", but I've cultivated it over the years. Craig says it is why I don't have a relationship and to that I say 'fuck you'. I dress nice for work and at home it's a miracle if pants get put on. T-shirt and jeans suit me fine, and a t-shirt sporting some awesome eighties icons from my childhood, well that's even better.

Then I did what most males do when they have a little time on their hands and happen to be alone, I rub one out. I avoided the time-sucking hole that is internet porn and just utilized my trusty spank-bank. It was a no-frills kinda masturbatory party, no pomp or circumstance, no solo foreplay just the bare mechanics of it all. Less fun, but gets the job done. Once clean-up is over, I head down to the garage of my building, fired up my barely ever used two-thousand and five Corolla and GPS'd my route to the campus.

The college is a mix of old architecture monstrosities and newer modern eyesores. The main buildings had been erected in the eighteen hundreds. They were gothic in nature, ornate and beautiful and spreading out from them were more modern buildings. Added over the years as the college's population increased. The whole place was like a mismatched table setting that somehow worked out beautifully in spite of itself. I knew a few movies had been filmed here. A few of them very serious coming of age dramas, but mostly they were gory killer on campus themed slashers. None of that knowledge helps me as I am completely lost as I stand in front of the main hall. The main quad is a hubbub of activity with students rushing to and from their classes. A small group is standing around listening as one girl rants about the testing of something on animals. She has hairy armpits that are braided, so I don't know who can take her ass seriously. A few frat boys are handing out flyers for a party later that evening. I also keep hearing chatter about some sports event. Whenever people talk about sports I completely tune out. They could, in the middle of their sports talk, give me all the answers to everything I ever wanted to know. But I'd be clueless. All I hear is "sporting sport sporty sports."

I quickly download the college's app to my phone which shows my location on the huge campus. I am around the academic buildings and to my left are the dorms. On my right are the athletic facilities and sports fields. Past that is fraternity and sorority houses, which are all gathered together in a little neighborhood of their own. I head to my left, the guy I'm supposed to meet, RJ is in Preston Hall.

As I move through the dorm's halls I think about how I missed out on the college experience. I opted to move out right away and go start my "should have been fabulous" life. Not that I'm complaining. I work for a successful magazine. I make a nice amount of money, live in the city and I have a great collection of friends. Yet I've always romanticized the idea of the college life I missed out on, until this very minute.

This dorm smells like an old, moldy, expired asshole. It is a pungent mix of dirty laundry, feet and old food all having a bareback orgy in a trash dump. My nose is being raped, and I withhold my urge to gag. I'm a little lost so I track down a student, hoping to see at least one hot college guy. All I find is a portly, pimply-faced fuck who has most likely never known the touch of anyone, except maybe his uncle, but even those days are long gone. He ain't making secret movies in Uncle Charlie's basement anymore that's for sure. He looks frightened to interact with another human being but directs me on how to get where I'm going. Ever see someone so hideously unattractive you can't help but wonder what sex with them would be like? Me either, let's move on.

In the hall, I pass an open door to one of the rooms. I shouldn't look but my admittedly pervy desire to see a little hot college man-flesh turns my head. Nope, not my luck this time, just three lonely nerds playing Dungeon and Dragons. I give them a dirty scowl for not being hot dudes changing clothes and move on. One of them pops his head out of the door and questions why I'm there. "Aren't you a little old to be here?" he asks all nasally, just living up to the fucking stereotype.

I resist the urge to go kick his ass just for the hell of it and smile instead, "Aren't you a little old to be a virgin? Go back to your circle jerk Fucktard."

Asian nerd retreats back into his room but not before flicking me off. Fucking kids, this is why I don't talk to anyone under thirty anymore. It's a good rule. Trust me when I say you should apply it to your own life immediately.

Finally, I turn the right corner and I find the correct room. I knock on the door. I'm nervous. I tap my pocket, I have plenty of cash. Let's just do this quick so I can go home. *Maybe he's really cute.* Or maybe he's another fucking nerd. This place seems to have more than its fair share of them. The door opens and before I can see who is behind it, his hand reaches out, grabs the top of my shirt and pulls me in.

I swear I'm lifted off my feet and I fly into the room. I could be exaggerating but that is what it felt like. I land on his bed, face first, and into a pile of dirty underwear. I know without looking that my body has scrunched up, so my ass is undoubtedly up in the air. Two seconds in a college guy's dorm room and I'm presenting myself like it's a fucking Nat Geo Wildlife special.

"Whoa, man, you okay dude?" A sweet, soft voice asks.

I take a whiff of the underwear. What? Maybe I liked it. Maybe I didn't, sure as hell not going to tell you pervs. I straighten myself out and push myself off the bed and come face to face with RJ, and goddamn he is ridiculously good looking. I'm not even joking about this. Staring at me is an Abercrombie and Fitch ad come to life. He is six foot three, full head of thick chestnut hair, gorgeous blue eyes and one of those killer smiles that would make it okay if he gave me Gonorrhea tonight. He's shirtless, so obviously there is a god and I thank her quietly. His chest and abs are mesmerizing, almost hypnotic. The play of his muscles as he moves is musical. I thought these kinds of good looks could only be achieved with Photoshop, yet here he is smiling at me.

"You're Derek, right?"

Yes, I am and say my name again baby, say it all night long, but I respond with; "Um yeah, RJ right?"

He smiles at me again and extends his hand which I shake. "Yeah man, nice to meet ya, any friend of Barney is cool with me."\

So, it would be cool if I ripped off your pants and sucked you so dry you had to be admitted to a hospital and placed on fluids?

"Sorry about the pulling, just getting amped up ya know." He bounces around his small single dorm room. No roomie for this hottie.

"Oh yeah? Is something going on tonight?
Like fucking me till I can't walk?
"I got big things tonight man." He moves around the cramped space with restrained yet still manic energy. "I could really use your help. I was so pumped when Barney said he was sending you over to meet me."

"Yeah about that," I interject, but he doesn't hear me. He's grabbed some dumbbells and is doing curls. I could faint, seriously.

"I really need some help tonight dude, big things tonight!" He emphasizes every word with a hand gesture. He is indeed pumped about something. I assume it's the sporting event I kept hearing mentioned. He drops the dumbbells and begins doing pushups. Watching the muscles flex in his back could cause me to have an aneurysm. I think my heart is palpitating, so I casually check my pulse just to be sure.

"You down for helping me, man? Won't be anything hard I promise."

Not hard? Listen fucker it better be all kinds of hard and pressing up against me in like twenty minutes. "Sure, no problem," is all I mumble out instead. He seems really nice and I really don't have anything to do. There's all night to get stoned and watch movies. Imperial China delivers until two a.m. on Fridays and Saturdays, so I got some extra time to help him.

"It'll be real quick and then I'll get your stuff, sound good?" He looks me right in the eyes and his face is so soft, so sweet, like the boy next door right out of a fifties movie who is so oppressively white you just know he is going to date rape you. Actually, his whole demeanor is sweet which is a bit unexpected since he has the outward appearance of the rough jock douche type.

But there is no sports paraphernalia anywhere in his room; no footballs lying around in the corners or baseball pendants tacked to the walls. No copies of

Sports Illustrated covering the floor. The room is small but very tidy, his bed is a mess with his dirty laundry – do you think he'd notice if I tucked a pair of his tightie-whities into my pocket for later?

There are textbooks on the desk and then a set of Harry Potter books on the dresser. really good looking, sweet guy who also reads Harry Potter? Um, please marry me.

RJ pulls on a blue polo that hugs his chest like a loved one hugging someone goodbye at the airport before a long flight. He tosses his phone at me. Dare I scan through it for naked selfies when he isn't looking? "I just need you to take the pics." He instructs me as he leans over and begins to show me how to work his phone. "Use the mode where it does video and pics at the same time. I hope you can capture all the action man, I need really good shots."

I'm not that old dammit, I know how to use a smartphone. "Sure, are you gonna model or something?"

"Yeah, it's something like that," he replies checking himself out in the mirror.

I get a view of his ass in the tight khaki pants and dear god, my anaconda don't want none unless you got buns hon – and he do. So mesmerized by his ass am I, that I'm not really paying attention when he turns to me with his pants undone and being held up by the waistband with just his finger.

"I'm gonna show you this now, so we get it out of the way because I don't want you becoming distracted while you're shooting me."

"I'm sorry, say what?"

He doesn't respond. He just drops his pants. I don't know if I imagine it or if he has an actual spotlight installed somewhere in his room for this exact moment. When he revealed what he had hanging between his legs I swear that area of him got brighter. Huge is not the right word, mammoth might be, maybe even colossal. It had to be twelve inches long, maybe thirteen, and as round as a beer can.

Look I've seen a lot and I mean A LOT of penises in my day, so I can spot a good one from twenty paces. This one is a gargantuan, magnificent piece of man-flesh. I didn't have my opera spectacles on me since I had left in such a hurry but had I would have whipped them out and taken a closer look. Instead, I just lean in with a little drool in the corners of my mouth. He has a tattoo running down the length of his shaft and a single word: PUNISHER, written out in block print and fully legible mind you despite his not being erect.

He pulled his pants up, caging up his beast. "So, you've seen him and now you can focus on what I'd like you to do."

"Dude, I don't think I'll ever be able to focus on anything again," I say not realizing that I had actually said it aloud.

He laughs, "Yeah I get that a lot. It's just a dick though."

"Man, my dick is just a dick. Yours is something else, like a piece of living penial art."

"Girls hate it, always complaining."

I stop myself before saying anything lewd. Those stupid bitches, I sure as hell wouldn't complain. Well, honestly, I probably would. Look the thing about a getting with a guy who has a huge dick is that it's all great in theory; Fun to talk about, fun to fantasize about but in reality, it never works out as you'd hope. Plus I don't want that thing near my secret garden, I'd be wrecked for days, nay-nay I say. But I don't shy from a challenge, so I'll gladly unhinge my jaw like an Anaconda and go down on it.

"Guys usually don't though, but they get too clingy"

Say what? Did the adorable cutie with a huge cock and ass that won't quit, just say he was Bi? Maybe my eyes lit up, or I made a squeal of delight because he quickly follows up his statement.

"But not right now, sorry, gotta save my energy for what needs to be done." He turns to his dresser and puts something I can't see into his pocket and then pulls out a lacrosse stick from his small closet. Dammit, it's sports. Why is it always fucking sports?

I follow RJ out onto the quad, he walks over to a golf cart and we jump on. A minute later we're cruising across campus. As we travel he talks about his studies, he's pre-med. He calls his mom every Sunday and they talk for an hour about their week. He has a girlfriend right now, but she wants to take a break. I tell him to enjoy the separation and fuck everyone he can. He just laughs and gets all shy, saying he can't do that. He really wants to like the person first and isn't into one-night stands, before adding that he changes his mind about that a lot because he gets very lonely sometimes. Oh, you adorable well-hung cutie, you can call me if you ever get lonely.

We pass the sports facilities, where I can hear and see some type of activity is going on. RJ doesn't slow down. We move the talk to movies. I tell him my plan for tonight and why I want the weed. He doesn't like horror movies, so instantly he's struck off of the potential boyfriend list. Dammit RJ you had to ruin what would have been a beautiful thing. I would have walked into the office Christmas party with him on my arm and make those bitches die with jealousy.

He turns a corner and we pull up on the street with the frat and sorority houses. He brings the golf cart to a stop and turns it off. He jumps out with the lacrosse stick across his shoulder. He shows me again how to use the video setting he wants and I assure him I'm ready for whatever it is we're doing. Hopefully, it's filming some home-made porn. I can't lie; I want to see the Punisher in action.

It is slightly eerie how the rows of frat houses and sorority's looks like it is a normal everyday neighborhood. I expect at any moment a scantily clad sorority girl to fun screaming by, chased by a masked maniacal killer. Or to see an epic frat kegger complete with togas and a donkey. Sigh, why is life not like the movies?

Tonight, it's super quiet and I'm like what the fuck, are they all studying? I follow RJ, he knows where he is going and he has a very determined look on his face as I follow along. He stops at one of the frat houses and looks around before going up the walkway. I could not tell you which one it was because, hell if I can read those Greek letters. RJ knocks on the door and reaches into his pocket.

I am glad that Barnabas, in his own way, pushed me out into the world tonight. He is always spouting off little bits of wisdom to which I usually call him a Hippie and go about my business. Tonight though, maybe he was right.

The door is opened by a very cute frat boy with sandy-blond curly hair. RJ pulls a black Taser gun from his pocket and shoots off the two electrodes into Frat Boy's chest before I have time to register what's happening. Then I see the boy's eyes widen at the crackling pop of the electricity shooting through the gun. Convulsing, he falls to the floor as RJ turns and flashes that killer smile at me.

Oh, Barnabas what in sweet gay hell have you gotten me into?

"His brothers are all at the charity football game," RJ assures me as we push the still convulsing Frat Boy into the living room. RJ turns him over onto his stomach and forces the boy's hips into the air, then using the boy's belt ties his arms behind his back. "So we've got enough time to have fun with him."

Frat Boy slowly comes to and looks around wildly at his new situation. "What in the fuck dude?"

RJ quickly slams the end of the Lacrosse stick on the hardwood floor centimeters from Frat Boy's head, which startles me and instantly shuts Frat Boy up. "Remember me?" He asks coming around and getting face to face with him.

Frat Boy shakes his head.

"You don't remember how you rejected me pledging your fraternity?"

"No man, I'm sorry."

"Sorry?" RJ stands up and looks at me, "Derek, he said he's sorry." He says motioning for me to start filming with the phone.

I start recording but can't help but find it very odd that RJ would be denied the option to pledge a frat since he seems like total frat material to me.

"You're sorry for rejecting me, but not for using me for my drug connections."

"You're crazy dude, that's why we didn't let you in!" Frat Boy shouts at him, immediately bracing for another whack of the lacrosse stick.

"Crazy?" RJ turns to the camera, "Is it crazy to be tired of this frat nonsense? This nepotistic filled, stereotypical cliché ridden bullshit excuse for a networking system all so someone's Daddy can give you a pity job after college."

"What the fuck you talking about bro?"

"Let's not forget anti-intellectualism, sure can't get a high GPA but can win at fucking beer pong can't ya?" RJ never yells, I notice that his voice only rises sharply for a moment then settles back down, but his rant is still filled to the brim with passion.

RJ reaches into his back pocket and pulls out a folded paper. "Submitted for approval, this frat brother's emails," he shows them off to the camera, "let's see how well he's spending his parent's money.' He begins to read: *"Subject, Rager Tonight. Listen up Fags, we're raging tonight, all fucking night. Let's get them Phi-Delta's drunk as shit and get those titties out. Hashtag, Free Dem Titties.'* Your parents must be so proud." RJ rolls his eyes and continues reading, *"We need handles of booze, who's buying? Get the pledges to make Jell-O shots. Phi-Delta's love motherfucking Jell-O-shots! Let's get this rage train on the tracks and let's all get our dicks sucked tonight one way or another."'*

Undoing his pants, RJ continues; *"Subject URGENT, Someone, in the next hour, needs to get in contact with that tall goofy motherfucker who hooks us up,"* RJ points to himself, *"'we need EVERYTHING for tonight, we're raging tonight– we're gonna kirk the fuck out and maybe, no WE ARE gonna get some pussy, hashtag Get Dat Pussy, It's my solemn goal that all my brothers get fucked up, and get laid – it's our fucking birthright as Kappa's to be getting laid every fucking party. Don't stop forcing drinks in those bitches hands until they can't fucking stand. It's there for you my Brother's so fucking take it"'*

He recites the last email as I watch his penis become fully erect down the inside leg of his khakis. *"'Subject Mixer, brothers, the Sorio-sluts Phi-Delta's are throwing a mixer. Everyone needs to be on fucking time, let's show them how we do. The pussy is for the taking brothers, so fucking take it. No only means maybe, so get some fucking drinks in them and watch them go. Pledges need to clean the house while we are at the mixers. Let's get our dicks wet tonight brothers."'*

RJ drops his pants fully, unleashing the Punisher. I see the look of fear in Frat Boy's eyes. But after those emails, I really kinda hate this douche.

"You're an entitled piece of date-raping shit, and you think you're better than everyone else. But are you bigger than me?" RJ stands right in front of Frat Boy's face. He holds out the Punisher for Frat Boy's closer inspection, "are you bigger than me?"

Frat Boy has tears welling up in the corner of his eyes, his face flushed, "no, look whatever the fuck you're gonna do, don't do it. We can rethink your pledging. We can skip the hell week nonsense. I can make you a brother."

RJ moves around behind him and yanks his pants down, revealing a pretty nice white round ass. I mean if anyone had asked my opinion about it. No one did of course, but I'm sharing it anyway since - it's fairly nice.

"Please man. Please don't do this, please."

"I thought it's your birthright to get fucking laid?" RJ spits into his hand.

Dear Jesus! He is going in prison-style! Is it wrong that this is so hot? I move in closer with the camera. RJ flexes his arms and poses, flashing me that smile again. It literally makes me swoon like a teenage girl at a boy band concert.

"I'm here to make sure you get laid." RJ grabs Frat Boy's hips and with no warning, slams the Punisher in. I keep the camera centered, I got one job here, but I can't help but cringe. That must hurt in a way I can't describe.

Frat Boy screams like he is being murdered. I mean can you blame him, he is technically being impaled. He is full-fledged crying at this point. RJ is unmerciful with the Punisher as he pounds for a good solid ten minutes. All the time posing as I take his picture, he's a natural in front of the lens. Frat Boy has his faced smashed against the floor, the area rug he is on muffles his cries and absorbs his tears. I try to capture the best shots, falling back on my untold hours of internet porn experience, I know how certain things should look for the viewer.

"UH-OH!" RJ yells, "Looks like we've hit some oil."

My stomach tightens. Even a delicate homosexual such as I know what he is referring too. There is no getting around it. When one has sex in the ass it occasionally happens. I too have encountered a sexual partner who is not as fresh and clean as they claimed to be. Then that moment when you've gone too far, and your cock returns with a little surprise - the dreaded Dookie Dick. RJ pulls out and the scent, though faint, hits the air. I can see *it* on the head of his penis and go to aim the camera elsewhere.

"No," he orders me politely, "I'd like you to capture all of this please." RJ quickly comes around to the front of Frat Boy and smears his dick across his upper lip. The fabled Dirty Sanchez. I don't think anyone ever needs to see it occurred in real life, but I've captured it on video so the world can see the shit smeared all over Frat Boy's face. He heaves and gags, unable to wipe his face as his hands are still bound behind his back. RJ repositions himself in front of the ass and continues his mission. Frat Boy has stopped screaming, he's closed his eyes and I know he is praying for all this to be over.

"Keep taking pictures," RJ requests nicely as he stops to pose for the camera, "Capture all of this, all of this retribution for everyone this entitled fuck has hurt." He's so at ease in front of the camera every pose is effortless. "I wish cell phones could have flashbulbs, how great would that be! This is for every girl you've forced in your bed, every pledge you've hazed cruelly, every student you've cheated off of because you've been too hungover or strung out to study." RJ is gearing up the momentum of his thrusts. I can tell he is close to bringing this bad boy home. Finally, he screams out in climactic ecstasy, "I AM THE RENEGADE RAPIST AND I FUCK FOR ALL OF THOSE YOU'VE FUCKED!"

There is one final extremely forceful penetration and it is over. RJ pulls all of himself out and pushes Frat Boy over onto his side, using his t-shirt to wipe the Punisher clean. Frat Boy vomits onto himself and pulls himself into the fetal position.

Still posing for the camera, RJ slides his pants back on and his natural boyish charm shows through, despite the kind of awful thing he just did. He walks over to me and grabs me around the waist and pulls me to him, giving me a quick kiss on the cheek. "You did an amazing job back there, really solid work, I know it's gonna look great."

I look into his eyes and I can't help it, he's so fucking adorable. I shuffle my feet. "Aww thanks, I mean I tried. You were an amazing subject to shoot very present and in the moment."

He squeezes me a little tighter and gives me a wink before releasing me. "Let's go."

We leave Frat Boy behind. Curled in the fetal position on the cheap area rug, his ass a bloody, shit smeared semen leaking mess and I can hear him bawling as we close the door and walk out in the cool night air.

I'm an accomplice now for sure.

I could have probably slid by without an arrest after that first offense. *"I didn't know officer. I was just caught up in the drama!"* That would be my main defense. Crying I would declare to them *"I got caught up in these runaway rapings!"* Maybe there'd be a trial, though I would not want RJ to get in trouble, but a good trial is always fun. Imagine a jury's face when they play the videos in the courtroom. Maybe one of them will faint outright at that Renegade Rapist line and I'm sure RJ would look handsome in a designer suit. As the charges are read he'll flash that smile and maybe even get off. I'd be a star witness of course, is there any other kind? It's nice to dream dreams, isn't it?

As we walk away from the third house on our Renegade College tour and have left yet another frat boy a broken, fetal mess on the floor. I fear denying any knowledge won't be very convincing. I'm an accomplice now no doubt about it and all I wanted was some pot, some movies, my couch and a weekend to my damn self. Thankfully I think we're done for the night. The newly dubbed Renegade Rapist and I walk back toward the golf cart. I don't know what came over me, I should have walked away from this mess, but the emails RJ read, the things those guys said and did. I couldn't help but feel a little, tiny, *well, not so tiny,* piece of justice was served. I resigned myself to bring this night to a close. Get the pot, go home, and lay low until the heat is off. Listen to me, *'lying low,' 'the heat is off,'* one hour as a criminal and I got the lingo down.

"Hey, motherfuckers!" The angry voice stops us in our tracks, and we turn around. About thirty feet behind us is a group of frat guys, or is it a gaggle? Maybe a school, or is it a flock? Whatever the classification for a gathering of douchebags was, it was now standing there. I could see our first stop from the tour; Frat Boy, out in front, wearing someone's comforter as a large homemade diaper. I can't help it and bust out laughing at the sight.

The tall dark-haired preppy looking foreman of the group points a baseball bat at me. "What's so funny faggot?"

RJ moves in front of me and puts his right arm out pushing me back, in that big brother protective move and am not going to lie, it made me wet. "There's no need to use that language, you got a problem buddy?"

"Yeah," Preppy Boy snaps back, "I got a big fucking problem. Paul here has to wear a fucking diaper. His ass has been leaking non-stop all over the fucking house, man. This," he points to the diaper, "is my duvet, three hundred thread count, ruined! And our living room, it's totally fucked! The smell of shit man, it's overwhelming. How are we gonna fuck girls in a shit smelling house dude? The fuck is wrong with you?" Paul taps Preppy Boy on the shoulder and whispers something in his ear. "Oh yeah, yeah, got it," Preppy Boy looks back at us, "and you fucking raped him, dude, what the fuck was that about?"

"He deserved it, and he probably liked it. I'm pretty sure your frat house is bursting with the repressed energy of your guys' latent homosexuality. Now you don't have to hide it anymore. Turn around, go home and give each other bro-jobs in your shit smelling man cave like the filthy ass bandits you are." RJ turns to me, "sorry."

"I've been called worse." It's true and by family no less.

"You're fucking dead man! No one talks to us like that!" Preppy Boy screams. His followers follow suit. Hurling threats to kick our asses and how we're gonna pay for what we've done. Plus a few 'Queer' and 'Fags' tosses in from their limited vocabulary.

"Thou doth protest too much," RJ shouts as he turns to me suggesting we run now and make a break for the golf cart. Fuck this shit, I'm not athletic, I was saving any running I had to do for the inevitable zombie apocalypse.

I barely make it to the golf cart, but I jump on the back just in time for RJ to pull away. He hands me the lacrosse stick and instructs me to whack a few frat boys if they get close. A golf cart is not exactly the fastest getaway vehicle and soon the horde of preppie assholes descends upon us. I summon all the masculinity I have and start swinging the stick. CRACK! I knock a big one upside his stupid head and he tumbles down, taking a couple of the others with him. Well, well if my father could only see me. Who's a sissy now Dad? I can see Paul all the way in the rear trudging along in his shit-stained three hundred thread count faux diaper. The golf cart gains a few feet between us and the frat.

"I should be honest with you," RJ shouts to me over the commotion.

"About what," I swing the stick wildly. SMACK! Nailed another one in the head, he goes down. The adrenaline is rushing through me. Maybe after all this is over I'll take up a sport. I feel so fucking alive!

"I, um, don't have any weed right now. I'm kinda dry." He looks back at me sheepishly. "I just really needed someone's help tonight and when Barney texted me it seemed kismet."

"ARE YOU FUCKING KIDDING ME?" I didn't want to yell at him but the situation called for it. I am going to possibly die tonight on this campus. "I can't believe this."

"I'm sorry Derek, really, and I've had so much fun with you tonight. I hope you still like me and maybe we can hang sometime."

Dammit as much as I want to be all Fuck You, I can't. He's so nice and sweet, and hot don't forget the hot part, it's very important. I cave, "Of course I'll hang with you, but they're going to kill us!" I point out the horde getting closer.

"No, they're not," RJ makes a hard-left turn, "they're not going to hurt my new forever friend!" He slams the brakes forcing the golf cart sideways and as it begins to tip over, I jump off and so does he. We have a brief moment behind the golf cart which is now lying on its side. "GO!" He shouts pointing to a walkway. I don't know where I am but I throw the lacrosse stick to him and make a run for it. "Go to Swine," he yells to me, "Find Bull the Null and he'll hook you up, I promise! Go now!" RJ stands up just as the frat descends on him. He whips the stick around with one hand, throws punches with other. Frat boys are going down left and right. It's truly a sight to see.

I take off down the walkway. I turn back only once to see my new beloved, the new star of my masturbatory fantasies. He has undone his pants and is using the erect Punisher as a weapon.

Eric David Roman

3: Female Trouble

The walkway, which thankfully no one follows me down, leads to a pretty long staircase. At the bottom of it, I realize I'm no longer on campus. I am actually back in the city. This means the walkway has led me to the opposite side of the campus, and very far from where I parked. The realization sinks in that it is now too far to hoof it and get back to my car. At least I'm not frat boy fricassee.

I look around at the surroundings. I am in a very quiet residential area. I start walking a couple of blocks just to ensure a good distance between me and the ruckus. I hope RJ is okay. I pull out my phone, which great, now has a cracked screen. Fuck! I'm one of those stupid twenty-something girls in line at Starbucks with their cracked iPhones. Seriously what the fuck are those girls doing that all their phone screens are always broken? Does no one buy the damn warranties?

My battery is getting low too, that damn campus locator app has drained it. I use my GPS and realize I am in L-Town, a quieter part of the city, nestled against the rear part of the college. Mostly residential townhomes with a few blocks dedicated to shopping and entertainment. It hasn't really been gentrified yet so it lacked a lot. It certainly wasn't the worst place to be lost in this city that's for sure. So now I'm stuck here and I need to figure out what to do. I doubt any cabs are around and calling for one would mean standing on the street corner for a half-hour or longer. I don't care to look like I'm here to give anyone a Z job thank you very much. The nearest subway, like my car, is probably too far to get to by foot. Do I even go home? My quest unfulfilled, my goal unattained. I google this Swine place RJ told me to go to. I'd never heard of it. I was pretty limited to staying within the same seven blocks around my apartment. Once you find a good bar that treats you right, you don't waiver your loyalty and go looking for better. Plus this city has so many places that come and go overnight.

Apparently, Swine is a gay bar. I still have never heard of it, but that's not saying much. It looks like it's not too far either. A bit of a walk but hey that's where the drugs are. So let me get to them first and then figure out a way home. I don't have enough battery life to actually use the GPS. So I try to memorize the route and I start on my way.

The night air is a little chilly so I'm glad I have my hoodie on. I make a left, go down a little hill past that famous cupcake place that always has a mile-long line. It leads me out to L-Street, the main strip of this little burg. It's a little past nine and most of the shops are already closed. The bars are not though and the Friday night crowds have gathered. As expected, people are milling out in front smoking. Which always fucking annoys me. Look I don't care that people smoke mind you. I do care that I have to walk through that cloud of smoke to get into and out of the bar. Seriously you can't just go a few feet to the left or right of the door? C'mon.

I walk past and give the polite head nod that says "hello, how are you, that's good" without actually having to vocalize it.

A couple of blocks down I turn off onto a side street and after a few minutes, I stop. I don't think I'm going the right way so I pull my phone out of my pocket about to check it when a hand grabs my arm and I get yanked into a club.

I am in a sleazy strip joint named "Udders", the graphic on the wall behind the coat check girl is a cow looking over its shoulder with tassels on it's you guessed it, udders. Beneath it, the moniker reads *Udder, Udder Delight!*

What in straight person hell is this?

The man who grabbed me introduces himself as Norwell. He's in his late fifties but still a tall, strapping dude with a heavy southern accent. He lets go of my arm and strokes it. "Sorry about that, look man I really need your help."

Seriously, is this some kind of fucked-up Déjà vu? "What kind of help, because I've already had a pretty rough night and -"

He cuts me off, "Jemma won't perform unless there are a certain number of men in the audience. She's very strict about this and I'm one short. This has never happened, but I got a club full of men who've come to see her and if she don't come out and perform then I have to refund all their covers. All of them." He clutches his chest at the thought, "I'll let you in free of charge, whaddya say?"

"Not really my scene man, sorry."

"Not your scene? Who doesn't wanna see some free pussy?"

I almost throw up in my mouth. "I'm a delicate homosexual sir, and most certainly do not want to see any pussy. Free or otherwise, thank you for the offer." I turn to leave.

"Free bar tab."

I spin back around, "so about this pussy?"

The sweet burn of rum as it hits my throat is heavenly. It isn't top shelf but it will do. I know what you are thinking, but only a fool turns down a free bar tab. I have a very simple rule in life; never, ever turn down a free meal, a free drink or a free fuck. Doesn't matter who is offering it. Norwell made good on his promise and I will loiter around drinking for free till this Jemma performs.

I've been to a few strip clubs in my day, a few really nice ones and a couple on more of the sleazy side. The sleazier ones being a lot more fun honestly. Though going with my straight friends can be a bit annoying. They will undoubtedly think it is funny to order me a dance. A stripper giving a gay guy a lap dance is their equivalent of busy work I'm sure. She knows this isn't gonna lead to more tips so what's her motivation and I am only worried about how close her vagina is getting to my face. It's not fun for either of us.

Udders, is the lowest on the low end of that scale. The main room is dimly lit, thankfully, but I can see the walls have painted some nausea-inducing pink color and all of it is dirty, I certainly don't want to touch anything, and my shoes keep sticking to the floor. I pray that it's just the residue of spilled drinks and not semen. Please not semen, I really like these shoes.

In the front, there's a large stage with two stripper poles on each side and a ratty hole-ridden gold lamé curtain behind them. Around the stage is a railing which puts about three feet between the stage and the men pressing up against it in panting anticipation. Then there are booths and tables against the left wall and to the right wall, I can see an alcove where there are tiny rooms, the champagne rooms I'm guessing? Though I'm sure this is the kinda place where the STD ridden girls just flop it out right at the table. I bet there is a daycare in the back for all their fatherless babies.

Udders clientele is certainly different, from what I've seen in other strip joints. No businessmen in suits or rowdy bachelor parties. No groups of college kids thinking they're hot shit because they have cigars shoved in their mouths and some of daddy's money to throw around. No, the clientele here is a bit on the, how do I put this delicately, lower end. I spot a lot of bikers, construction workers and garbage men still in their work garb. Plus a few others but mainly all of them look a little on the grungy side. The place is packed, some are sitting, but most are standing around the stage. I can barely move and don't know what's so special about Jemma, but she sure demands a full house. Would she really know if I wasn't here?

On the stage now however is Stretch-Mark Sara. Yes, that's her real name because that's how she was announced to the stage. She comes out to some K-Pop song with high pitched Korean girls singing loudly about who knows what. It could be a terrorist manifesto and we'd never know as she flings off her K-mart bought sensible wear nightie and reveals her almost naked body. Thankfully a miss-matched bra and pantie set cover up a little bit of it. She lives up to her name, across her milky white skin are the darkest, widest, and deepest stretch marks I have ever seen. She dances for the men who are howling at her and throwing one-dollar bills. She licks her fingers then trace them along her stretch marks and it drives them wild. I can only stare on in horror as Sara slides off her bra and her rather large bosoms seem to deflate. With the bra on, she looked as perky as teen, but now its two deflated flesh colored balloons that are clinging onto her chest for dear life. She lifts them up, showing off the stretch marks along their sides.

I slam my drink. The quickly order another one, reminding them of Norwell's instructions. To my left is a long-haired guy who looks like he hasn't showered in a while and to my right is a guy with awkwardly shaved facial hair. He was apparently trying to craft a desired unique look but was drunk and it just went all to hell and now he looks like an abstract painting. I turn back and face the stage, Sara has removed her panties – Houston we have full beaver. Thank god I didn't have that Chinese food yet. She keeps spreading *it* open and sticking out her tongue. It looks like a gutted hedgehog and I suck down this second, very strong, rum and Coke to wash the memory of what I've seen. I probably should have eaten something, but fuck it, I order another one.

Awkwardly Shaved Facial Hair turns to me, "isn't it unfair how those of us who wanted to get molested never did? I tried and tried. Every Sunday I waited after mass but it never happened for me. Timmy Renault was the lucky one. Guess he was just more attractive."

Who the fuck starts a conversation like that?

The club is too packed for me to move away from him. I'm trapped – much like I imagine little Timmy Renault was at the hands of Father Bad Touch. He pulls out his wallet, opens it and shows me a picture of himself as an eight-year-old child.

"Do you think I was attractive enough to get molested?"

I do not believe there is a correct answer to this question so I look at the picture, "Yes you looked very fuckable." This seems to bring a smile to his face. I swear if he starts jerking off to his own class picture I am out of here, free bar tab or not.

Sara and her stretch-marks have finished their set. She waddles around the stage collecting her money.

Flicking off the guys who are cat-calling her then blowing them kisses. Timed perfectly when she leaves the stage, the lights go down and the crowd erupts in hoots and hollers. The scratchy voiced announcer gives a smoker's cough into the mic before he announces the next performer. "Here she is, that one-ton beauty, that goddess of the buffet line, the girl who'll tickle your pickle, then eat it...Jemma!"

Jemma the Jiggler storms her way to the stage to SIA's hit pop song *Chandelier*. Dear god all mighty, she's over 400 pounds. She has a really round face with long, stringy blond hair and no neck, seriously no visible neck like a giant thumb with a face and a wig on. She stands on the end of the stage and does one move - but all of her moves in opposite directions. Some of her rolls fly upways, some downways, some sideways, crossways, diagonal ways – I mean she's a fucking Wonkavator of a person and this crowd of degenerates adores her. She is wearing a purple brassiere with tassels. Those tassels, well they just add to the majesty of it all. I think there is a matching bottom but I, um, can't see it. Her folds are numerous.

I have to give it to her though, she loves her body. On stage, she shimmies, lifts up some of the folds and makes intense, sexually charged eye contact with the men in the audience. They make it rain dollar bills, but Jemma cannot bend down to pick them up. Instead, a very unhappy looking elderly guy, with an unlit cigarette hanging out of his mouth and ratty grey hair moves around the stage collecting it for her.

I watch in horror as she moves to the pole, grips it and heaves up her body so she can spin around on it, right on cue with SIA stating she wants to swing from that said chandelier. I think, very faintly, I hear the metal scream. The pole has to be reinforced in some way because it holds her up. Maybe lug nuts? The tasseled bra flies off into the crowd. The three men who catch each take a piece and rub against their faces, clearly achieving some kind of orgasmic thrill from it. As disturbing as those biker's O-faces are, Jemma's immense breasts are a stomach-churning sight. She lifts them up to her mouth and licks her own nipples, the areolas of which are as huge as pancakes, and disturbingly dark. She grabs both of her breasts and starts licking like a woman possessed. I will never eat at an IHOP ever again.

The crowd is in a legitimate frenzy and every time that mountain of flesh moves an inch they lose their shit. Now they've started chanting her name: Jemma! Jemma! Jemma! She gives them the look because she knows what they want as her body gyrates to the music. Another spin on the pole and then BAM – a full split, her legs stick out from under her fat like two tiny twigs caught in a flesh avalanche.

Thankfully that appears to be the end of her set. The elderly dude and another random stagehand appear and help hoist Jemma back up on her cankles before she shimmies once more for her audience and retreats back behind the curtain. The next dancer, Varicose Vera is announced. She's sixty-seven, gray-haired and her legs look like a topographic map of Asia.

I eye my exit strategy: ninja my way through this rowdy, very horned up crowd and slide out the exit and get on my way to Swine. I finish my drink, which will be my last because I'm pretty buzzed. One more of these and I might start hitting on this bunch of rough trade or at least rub up against their boners as I head out. I leave a tip because even though they're free drinks, I'm a fucking gentleman.

I'm stopped by Norwell just as I squeezed past some very hairy, fat, sweaty bikers and can just see the exit within my reach. He thanks me for my help and then tells me Jemma has asked that I come backstage. "She always allows a few fans to come back after her set."

"I'm not a fan. Really shouldn't someone else go?" Like Awkward Facial Hair Guy, hasn't he had enough disappointment in his life?

"She requested you," Norwell explains in a way that makes it clear it is not an invitation I can reject. Eh, what the hell, I've never met a stripper close up before. I follow Norwell as he moves past the stage. Vera is giving it her all; rubbing her veiny legs sexually while making oh's and ah's and licking her lips to the audience.

He leads me behind the stage where it is not as loud, the crowd and the music are muffled back here. Heading down a dark hallway, we pass what appears to be the dressing rooms. Stretch-Mark Sara is standing in the doorway of one of them totally naked, smoking and looking very angry, even though an apparent "fan" is suckling on one of her tits.

"This crowd is bullshit, I made barely anything. I'm sick of that fat heifer getting all the attention around here. These bring the boys in too ya know!" She motions to her namesakes. Norwell just throws up his hand and moves past her.

We pass a couple of more empty rooms until we come to the last one in the hall. Jemma's dressing room. Not the star treatment style I was expecting. It was narrow but still roomy with a chaise lounge against one wall, an eyesore with its bright red fabric. A large framed changing screen sits against the opposite wall with Jemma's huge bra hanging from it. There is a vanity with a makeup station. I was so overtaken by the sight on the stage. I didn't even bother to notice she had made herself up all pretty. There is a table covered by a sheet and three other men already in there. They stand silently against the wall waiting. Norwell doesn't enter he just ushers me in with his hand and leaves back down the hall.

I stand around wishing I'd still had my drink. It's uncomfortably quiet and I avoid eye contact. The three other men, one rough-looking biker, another who seriously has to be homeless, and the third a relatively cute guy wearing a suit. An expensive one if my GQ subscription has taught me anything. He and I look out of place here, but his face reads with anxious excitement.

We hear her voice first, loud and booming demanding a clean towel. The other men go giddy like children waiting to see their presents on Christmas morning. She enters wearing a white see-through nightie that barely comes up to her waist.

I watch Jemma move through the room. Frankly, I don't know how her ankles, keep all that body mass upright. Let alone accomplish the acrobatic act she just performed on the stage. I am scared to move. Maybe her eyesight is based on movement like the T-Rex and she'll gobble me up in a single swooping motion, having mistaken me for a McDonald's apple pie. None of the other men speak but their wide eyes follow her every movement.

"I'm gonna be a size six" she cries triumphantly, breaking the silence in the room. The men shout out in disapproval. They complement her beauty begging her not to lose any weight.

I, however, have has three fucking drinks so what do I do, I blurt out, "Um, how so?" The other men turn to me, eyes burning, shocked that I've spoken in the presence of their Goddess.

Jemma looks over at me, her eyes run up and down my body, and I now I know feel like an appetizer dish at T.G.I.Fridays. "By my diet silly boy," she giggles and moves toward the table covered with the sheet. She sits down at the table and pulls off the sheet revealing little jars all lined up. I recognize the smiling cherub faces on them instantly. It is baby food. She opens a jar

of the mashed peas and sucks it down. "I'm gonna be as
thin as an Olsen twin!" she declares, "Just wait and see."
The gooey slop clung to her face like mountain climbers
hugging a cliff. She moves from jar to jar getting more
on her than in her. And the noises, oh lord the noises.
There are no words to describe the noises she makes as
she sucks it down, but I think she is having an orgasm. I
love food too but come the fuck on.

After emptying ten jars of the food, most of
which now resided on her ample chest, she comes out
from behind the table and opens her arms. "Come eat
boys, Momma's here for you."

The three guys nearly push each other out of the
way to get to the meal and start licking the baby food off
of her. They bury their faces in the pureed buffet of peas,
bananas, and carrots all on her chest. I of course refrain,
watching in disbelief as the men go to town.

"Don't you wanna eat baby?" Jemma asks in her
best impression of an Anna Nicole style breathy voice.

"No, I'm good thank you."

The three men stop and look at me crossly. I can
see in their eyes they are angered I am here. I've invaded
their sanctuary. I want to vocalize that I did not ask to be
back here voyeuristically spying on their intimate
moment. But I don't, "Look I really enjoyed your show,
but I gotta get going."

"You can't go yet, Baby." She pushes the other
three men off of her. They have cleaned her up pretty
well at this point too. "See every night I pick a lucky
fellow to be my special companion." The men around her
start pleading for it to be them, but her gaze is fixed
intently on me. "I pick you. I saw you from the stage,
with that adorable face,"

She has a point, I'm seriously fucking adorable.

"And your cute little body."

Awe, she called me little. Compared to her I'm an anorexic skeleton, but I'm going to take the compliment.

"I want you to be my lover tonight." She rubs her hands all over her body, as she moves toward me. "All of this will be yours."

I can feel the hateful looks from the other men. "Um, so little problem," I dodge her and dart around her toward the opposite end of the room, and away from the exit like a fucking idiot. "See I'm gay, and I while I love women, I'm not big on the having sex with them part, even beautiful ones like yourself." A little flattery might get me out of here.

This stops Jemma, but not in the way I was hoping. Her eyes light up. "A FAG!"

"Whoa," I snap, "that word is harsh, just gay will suffice, thank you."

"I've always wanted to fuck a fag and I'm getting all wet now just thinking about it." She rubs her hand between the huge rump-roasts she calls thighs and then brings it to her mouth licking it.

So much is making me want to vomit tonight.

The guys start telling her they're gay as well. "I'm a fag. I suck the best cock," the suited one proclaims. "Just got finished with one before I came to see you, you can still smell the man jam on my breath!" He opens his mouth as to say 'see I'm telling the truth'.

She does not pay any attention to them, ushering them to be quiet with her hands as she is fixated on me.

"Well you can't really fuck us, that's, what makes us queer. I like dick." I back up to the farthest wall and realize there is nowhere else for me to go. There's a window about a foot above my head and Jemma's massive girth and her groupies standing between me and the door. Who's to say if I even make it to the exit that one of these goons won't try to stop me from leaving? If they're willing to suck half-eaten baby food off of her,

I'm sure they're more than happy holding me down while she rapes me.

"I have toys. I'll wear a strap-on! I'll show you pleasures like you've never known."

"Well first off, kinda rude to just assume I'm a bottom. I've pounded my fair share of ass. Besides, I've never done it with a lady, and I don't think I'd be any good at it. Also, I've had like three really strong drinks, so uh-oh whiskey dick." I smack at my crotch, "you won't get anywhere, it's like a taffy pull down there right now."

"You're a virgin then? A virgin fag! Don't worry baby, Momma Jemma will show you all you need to know. We'll take a guided tour of this candy shop."

"It's called being a Gold Star Gay actually, and I'd really, really like to keep my star." Seriously I would. I have no desire to sleep with a woman. I know some gays who get drunk and wander into the lady cave. Then they accept a Bronze star from the queer committee of elders. Not me, no sir, I'm all dick all the time. Except I mean, if I had to lose my precious star, I plan on losing it to Anna Kendrick. Not that she'll have me of course and am I aware of this, but she is so beautiful and so funny – have you read her twitter? I picture us cuddling on the couch watching movies, and I harass her until she does the cup song for me. Anna is the first legit lady crush that I've had since the mid-nineties when I questioned my sexuality after seeing Gillian Anderson on the X-Files. Even today she is still stunningly beautiful, I mean have you seen *Hannibal*? Thankfully though, David Duchovny's dreaminess was also there in the nineties, with those smoldering good looks to keep me grounded firmly in my homosexuality. *David Duchovny, why won't you love* me?

Jemma snorts, which snaps me out of my head. "You're losing that star tonight cutie, Jemma wants what

Jemma wants." She begins to kick her feet back like a bull. "And Jemma wants herself a SHINY GOLD STAR FAG!"

I kick her in the cunt.

I am not proud of it.

It wasn't the most gentlemanly moment of my life.

But when I saw her charging for me with the deranged look of sexual conquest in her eyes, I had to do something. In those split seconds that I saw that whale of a woman coming for me and my little gold star, it was the only thing I could think of. So, I threw out my right leg, used the Force to guide my foot right into her thermal exhaust port.

I wasn't sure at first if I had actually hit her cunt. How could you tell with all the folds of blubber? I could have just hit one of those and lost my sneaker or even my foot. She would laugh at my feeble attempt and then overpower me. Straddle my tiny hips and break my poor body in her attempt to get my untarnished gold star. But I hit that cunt alright, square on the nosey. I saw her beady eyes cross in shock as she made a loud whimpering sound, grabbed at her clam and went down like a ton of bricks. Literally, I think the building shook when she did. I wasn't sure if I had stunned her, knocked her out or even killed her and also, I didn't care.

With no time to waste, and the other guys already rushing toward her to help and probably coming for me next, I jump on her back, which acts like a trampoline and gives me the boost I need to get to the window. I didn't know where it would lead, but I knew we were still on the first floor. Pushing it open, I grab the ledge and propel myself out into the night air.

4: Multiple Maniacs

What was it Barnabas had texted me earlier? Oh yeah, '*The only way to live life is to go along with where it takes you.*' Well, Barnabas, this is where life has taken me. I'm lying in a dumpster. I kicked a lady in her hairy clam taco and now I'm lazing around on what one can only assume is stripper trash. Wonderful, just fucking wonderful.

The window that I used to flee Jemma's dressing room was higher than I thought. The building was actually next to an alleyway that went below street level and, in my daring escape, I tumbled out and fell about two stories. Luckily this dumpster was here, lid open, to catch my fall. By the grace of whatever deity is handling me and my shenanigans this evening, there's nothing gross on the top of the trash heap where I landed, just bags.

I've decided, however, that I'm just gonna stay here. Going to remain sedentary and look up at the stars as I ponder my existence in the world and wait until morning. Once the sun rises I'll text everyone I've ever met until someone comes to find me and takes me home. I'm seriously not moving. The decision has been made until I hear a rustling in the dumpster with me, I sigh loudly, because of course. I look over to see the wiggling tail of a rat diving deeper into the trash.

Fuck my life.

I grab the side of the dumpster and pull myself out. I'm a bit sore from my fall but I'll walk it off. I look up at the open window. No one is sticking their head out, and I can't hear any yelling. No demands for my body to be brought back and robbed of my precious gold star. Probably best to move quickly before that behemoth regains her composure and decides to come after me. It is only natural after getting kicked in the cunt to seek vengeance, or at least I am assuming. I think that's what *Kill Bill* was all about. Either way, I'm moving. I turn to run and come face to face with the end of a gun.

"What are you?" A stern, yet kind, British voice says. It takes me a moment to see the tall man holding the gun that is pointed in my face.

"I'm a delicate homosexual sir, who's having a bit of a rough night."

The man begins laughing. "That's a good answer." He lowers the gun from my face, "no need to worry, it's just a tranquilizer dart gun."

What the fuck goes on in this city after dark, seriously?

He steps under a street light. He's in his sixties, bald-headed with soft features. He looks like a teacher type, though he is dressed as some kind of urban version of Indiana Jones. "I'm Professor Alfred Randall-Esquire-Buzzington."

"That's a lot of names."

"Yes, I suppose it is." He looks off into the distance thinking about all his names. Has no one ever told him having four was a bit much? I look back at the dressing room window, I can see movement. The

Professor notices my uneasiness. "Are you in need of assistance young man?"

"Indeed I am Professor. I need to get away from here and I'm trying to get to a club called Swine."

"I can most certainly assist you in leaving the vicinity, and perhaps get you closer to your destination."

It seems my luck is changing.

"If you don't mind assisting me a little along the way."

Goddamit.

I cannot catch a break. I hesitate for a moment then reluctantly agree. I don't know why everyone in this damn city needs my help tonight, but I want to get away from Udders and Jemma, so I'll do what I have to.

The Professor leads me through the alley to his large white utility van. The kind I always see construction workers driving, with that huge Master lock on the side. What is he doing out in the city with such a huge, terrorist looking van?

I jump in the front and notice the back of the van is totally dark. I can't see anything past the front seat but I can hear a rustling noise from the back. I just spin around looking out the windshield, whistling *The X-Files* theme softly. I don't give a shit what this man is into. As long as he doesn't want to do anything crazy to me, like eat Cheerios out of my butthole. I'm just going to go with the flow.

Professor Buzzington gets in and lays the tranq gun between us. He starts up the van and we zoom through the alley then out onto the street. I am so terrible with locations that again I have no clue where I am. I really need to go exploring the city I live in. My safe haven seven-block bubble be damned.

"I'm an anthropologist," he announces to me after a couple of quiet minutes.

"You teach over at the college then? I was just there, pretty rough place."

"Well, not anymore, I'm on a sabbatical. My newest research project scared them and we couldn't see eye to eye anymore. I have tenure though so they can't fire me."

He takes a few turns at a pretty high speed. I hear more rustling in the back but ignore it and focus on the professor.

"What is your new research? I don't really know anything about anthropology except you dig up old places."

He slams his fist on the wheel. "A common misconception, it is the study of the living species that is Homosapien! What makes us tick, our social mores, our cultural attitudes. Everything that makes us tick dear boy, everything! My current area of interest is cultural anthropology, mainly focusing on social organization and culture change."

Wonderful, this guy isn't weird. He is just going to bore me to death. *You could be with Jemma.* I remind myself, and I let him talk on.

He slams the brakes. "LOOK!" he shouts as he moves the car to curb. He rolls down the windows as he points out a group of friends. There are five of them, all walking together down the sidewalk. "The one in the front, he's what we call, The Yelper."

I look toward the average, slightly chubby but still good looking guy who seems to be leading the pack. He is concentrating on his phone, the red background of the Yelp app reflecting on his face. I can hear them through the van's speakers. Buzzington points to the roof and tells me there is a microphone attached that he's now pointed at the group.

The friends are all whining about wanting to eat, which I can't help but find really odd. They're walking down a street that literally has five places to eat right in front of them. I turn to Buzzington, he motions for me to remain quiet but to keep observing.

"It's getting late dammit, Dave!" One frustrated member of the party chides loudly.

Dave, the leader, looks up and shakes his head to which, the group lets out a combined moan.

"The Yelper will not allow his pack to find nourishment," Buzzington's soft, British voice in my ear makes it sound like I'm watching an episode of *Planet Earth*. "Until the app alerts him he has found the correct watering hole that will nourish all of their needs."

I can't lie. It is fascinating to watch this unfold. Dave's group is starving. I can tell by their pinched angry faces, constant grabbing of their stomachs and the vile way they snap at each other. These bitches are next level Hangry and he seriously will not let them eat. One girl points to the pizza place and is shot down, hard.

"It has one star Julie, ONE FUCKING STAR! You think we're gonna eat in a place that has one fucking star?" Dave waves his phone in her face so she can see the one-star rated page. The others turn on poor Julie, berating her for her suggestion. And another girl snaps and calls her a stupid whore. Poor Julie, a hungry bitch has no friends.

"The Yelper can keep his pack hungry and on the verge of starvation for hours as he scours the local terrain for that perfect meal coming from the ideal mixture of 'stars' and 'good reviews'. He is an unquestionably low level of asshole."

One of the guys points to the Thai restaurant a few feet ahead.

"Yelp says the service is bad. We're not eating in a place where the service is obviously bad. Why are you so stupid Carl?"

"That's just one dude's opinion," Carl protests.

This is a mistake and is quickly addressed by the pack. The vicious verbal abuse that poor Carl takes is unmerciful. I cannot hear all of it, but within a moment he has been backed up against a building and is now sliding down the wall in tears tv movie style.

Dave goes back to his phone, the other members of the pack too frightened now to move or speak. Julie and Carl's punishments were warning to the others. Dave's fingers scroll down as he shakes his head at every option coming up. One of the girls spots a street vendor selling hotdogs and goes to say something but stops herself. "Clever girl," I whisper.

Buzzington leans over me and aims the tranq gun at Dave. "I don't normally intervene like this," he fires a dart that lands successfully into its target.

Dave grabs his neck and pulls the dart out. He looks around for only a moment before he drops his phone and topples over. The pack looks around wildly, unsure of what to do without their leader.

"You're free now!" Buzzington yells, "go forth and EAT!"

They look over at us for a stunned moment and then smile. They turn and run wildly into the Thai restaurant. Through the window, I can see the famished friends attacking other patrons. Snatching food off of their plates and shoveling it into their own mouths. Carl punches a waiter who steps over to try to stop them and then devours a plate of Drunken Noodles stolen from the table of a terrified woman who watches in horror. I am so enamored with the scene playing out in the restaurant. I don't notice Buzzington isn't in the van until I see him running up to the sidewalk and grabbing Dave by the legs. I jump out and rush over to help him.

"In the back," he instructs me, "I'll add him to the collection."

We toss Dave's body into the back of the van and close the door. I know now what the rustling was I heard earlier, and I will continue to ignore it. I can't help but think, *once again here I am, the merry accomplice doing what I can to help out strangers with their illegal acts.* Maybe that will be the title of the true-crime book they will write about me after all of this is over. 'The Merry Accomplice: the twisted tale of Derek Collins and his insatiable urge to accomplice.'

Buzzington puts his hand against my chest and the action instantly stops my mind from rambling, as you may have noticed by now it tends to do. He taps his tongue to the tip of his forefinger and puts it out in front of him. His eyes dart back and forth. "Time to press on," he heads over to the driver side of the van.

As we maneuver through the city the Professor explains the number of cultures, counter-cultures and sub-counter cultures he has studied over the years: The Goths who evolved into the "Emo's" – "less eyeliner, more attitude." Vegans - "hippies who took it too far." They're assholes because they're hungry and are never invited to dinner parties.

"I've become so engrossed in the way smartphones and social media have forced an evolutionary change in their own way. Creating an anti-social movement of people, who retreat into their devices to avoid personal contact. Or the social media narcissists who document every moment of their mundane lives for countless people to see and read. From my standpoint, it is absolutely fascinating."

I couldn't argue with the man. Especially since fake texting to avoid talking to people in the office, or in a line is one of my favorite recreational activities. "They've made people pretty rude too," I add, "nothing pisses me off more than when someone pulls one out in the middle of a fucking conversation. I can't be one of those people who are constantly on their phones avoiding the rest of the world."

"Indeed, such rudeness is intolerable. I've noticed you've not touched your phone since we've been together, even during the lulls in conversation. I must say it must be some kind of record for someone your age."

"Eh, the battery is almost dead, plus there is no reason to be on it anyway. I am in such good company." Hopefully, that will ensure I stay on his good side so I don't end up in the back. Plus, it is also a little true, the Professor is nice, very smart and appears to have no desire to eat Cheerios out of my butthole. I see this as a win.

It dawns on me I could have been live-tweeting this whole evening. It could be one of those tweets that go global and ends up an article on Buzzfeed. I'd be a Twitter "celebrity", which is like saying you're a real detective because you've won at Clue.

Buzzington brings the van to an abrupt stop and pulls gently over to the curb.

"Another prime example, observe," he motions over to the sidewalk, where I see a group of young girls stopped in the middle of the sidewalk. They're taking selfies of their evening attire before heading into a random bar. "The Selfie taker: modern society's newest and most annoying inhabitant."

He could not have been more right. I can't stand people who do nothing but take selfies every minute of the damn day. Clogging my social media feeds with nothing but their stupid looking mugs, staring at me with that vacant expression. Like they don't know where the fuck they are or how a camera got there. Here I am me at work. Oh, I'm so bored. Here's me in bed - I don't wanna start the day, sad emoticon. Here's me at a red light, cause driving is somehow making me look sexy as fuck today. No one fucking cares! We are just scrolling right by you, you vain motherfuckers. And furthermore, you should be driving the damn car not taking pics of yourself. The fuck wrong with you?

Nudes are okay though. DM me.

This group of girls has blocked off the sidewalk, not allowing anyone to pass by them as they take and retake pics trying to find that one perfect that pleases the entire group. "Use the beauty filter!" One demands. "Tilt it up, no at an angle, we'll look thinner!"

The middle girl then pulls a telescoping pole out of her purse – a selfie stick. She attaches her phone to the end, the other girls around her squealing in delight. "Tilt it up, tilt it up!"

I grab the tranq gun from the middle console, aim it and fire it into the leg of the annoying twit holding the selfie stick. Not knowing what is happening to her as the toxin races through her body. She begins to flail her arms and swings the selfie stick wildly, successfully smacks all of her friends in their faces. A blonde girl at the end receives the brunt of the first blow - it breaks her nose. Grabbing at the bloody mess, she trips in her high heels and goes headfirst into a garbage can. The stick swings back in the opposite direction careening into the brunette's head, who stumbles backward into a group of smokers outside the bar. They let her fall to the ground unwilling to drop their cigarettes to help, returning to their conversation once she was on the ground. The two girls directly on either side of the Selfie Twit both get punched in the face as Selfie Twit flings out both hands before she falls backward, taking her two friends down with her.

I set the tranq gun down and apologize, but the Professor is smiling to himself. We jump out and grab her and her annoying stick. We toss her in the back of the van and speed off. I think I could hear the witnesses on the sidewalk applauding our efforts as we pull away. I resist the urge to wave at them.

We continue to drive around and The Professor asks what I'm doing out this evening. I explain to him my grand plan for the evening and how it has gone awry with my soon to be ex-boyfriend the Renegade Rapist, and then the deranged stripper.

"There are a lot of crazy people out here, doing crazy things."

Yeah, Professor, you are right about that.

He talks a lot about the Millennials. As he does, I do the math in my head. I realize that most studies agree that the generation known as Millennials, begins in eighty-one. Dammit, and I've tried so hard to not be an asshole. The Professor assures me that annoyance lies in the younger ones. They're entitled and narcissistic, and apathetic. It's that apathy that according to the good professor is changing the world. "You see, they don't care about who wants to get married, or who wants to get high, so why make any of it against the law. So if they do actually vote, their voting contradicts the older generation views and that is changing the world. But like any younger generation, they're still annoying in their own way."

We park at a couple of different spots but never come across anyone for his collection. Not that he verbalizes this of course. A few times I could have sworn I see a brown van stopped at a couple of the places we are stopped at. It was very recognizable, a dark brown seventies-era conversion van. I bet it has shag carpeting in the interior. On more than one occasion I thought I saw people being loaded in the back of it. I brush it off as a ridiculous notion until I remember what I was assisting the Professor with

The Professor is quiet for long periods, seemingly lost in his own head, until he would blurt out random things. "There are two groups of people. There are the ones who wipe their bottoms while still sitting on the toilet, and then those who wipe it while standing up."

What the fuck?

"And until I've just told you that, you never knew about the other group, did you?"

He was right. I wipe whilst still sitting like the delicate homo I am, but apparently, there are people who do it standing up and I can't fully process that information. Why would anyone stand up to wipe their ass? Remain seated, wipe, and flush all before getting up. This is partly to remain safely out of visual range of the unpleasantries, and partly because I'm lazy.

"See the complexity of our crazy world, more than you ever thought I'm sure."

I'm now questioning everyone I've ever met, do they wipe sitting or standing. I think I'll have to renew friendships based on this piece of new information.

"We are at a crossroads.' His voice breaks my concentration. "I can go left and follow one route that will bring us close to where I believe you said you reside, or I can follow my original plotted course which will take us by the aforementioned club Swing. I leave it up to you dear boy."

I think of my quiet apartment. My comfy lounging clothes my couch. It is close to eleven-thirty now and I have been up since six A.M for work. The evening has not gone as I had planned thus far and I could call it quits, admit defeat go home and think nothing more of it. Drink that bottle of vodka in my freezer and drift off to sleep or, I could go to Swine. Meet this Bull guy, get my dope, have a drink and hang out at the club until I find a cab to take me home. Then retreat into my apartment and get stoned watching movies.

They are both solid plans. One just involves reaching my bed faster. Look I'm thirty-four, not twenty-four, my up all night party days are long behind me. My friend Cecil will call sometimes at around ten-thirty or eleven to tell me he's just now going out and asks me to go along to some random bar or club.

I hang up on his ass.

Go out at ten-thirty?? I say nay-nay! I need to already be out and about by that time or am in. I mean I am as in as in can be.

Oh fuck it, sometimes you have to go where life takes you right? I've come this far so I tell the Professor to turn right. He agrees I've made the correct choice. Apparently, I'm doing something right tonight since I'm in the front of the van and not in the back.

We are a couple of blocks away from Swine when he pulls over and jumps out. He taps the tip of his finger to his tongue again and points it out into the night sky. His eyes light up.

I look around the area we are in. Two organic markets, several thrift stores, and a record store – it can mean only one thing...

"Hipsters!" he proclaims excitedly.

I don't see any but I trust the mad man next to me, so they must be around. I do spot someone across the street, and for a moment I don't believe it.

"My god"

"Is that what I think it is?" I ask.

He shushes me as to not scare him away. There across the street leaving an apartment building and an apparent time machine as well. It is a Grunge, straight from the nineties themselves. The long hair that was clearly unwashed. The blue jeans with large but not fully ripped holes in the knees. A red and black flannel shirt tied around his waist, and a now vintage, ripped, Nirvana t-shirt. I think I went to school with that guy, hell anyone my age went to school with this fucking guy.

"He is a rare sight indeed, as most of the Grunge have evolved. We must not interfere," Buzzington explains, "any sudden motions could send him back into his nest. They can be skittish."

"Where is he even going? Do any bars even play that music anymore? This isn't Seattle."

"His social group long ago abandoned their ways. Too old to be a hipster, if he attempted he would be accused of trying too hard and shunned viciously. He is a lone wolf in unfriendly terrain. He will move to other groups, finding solace in them for a short period of time. Trying to assimilate into their way of life, but he will always end up alone."

Grunge guy wanders past, both of us staring at him wide-eyed and mouths agape until he turns a corner and leaves out of sight. It was like seeing a Unicorn.

"Rare indeed," Buzzington looks past me and grabs my arm in a rush of excitement.

I hear them before I see them.

"I told him that my art is not classifiable. It is an ironic look at an un-ironic state of being as interrupted through the looking glass of the dexterity of social media's everyday working man."

The Hipsters are coming up the sidewalk. One is tall, lanky and of some sort of Asian descent. I'm sure if I asked him he'd give me some line about being of "pan-Asian ancestry but doesn't like to be classified by labels." His outfit is an atrocity - tight multi-colored paisley leggings, bright blue sneakers, a soft pink tank-top with grey suspenders, and an apparent woman's hideous plaid design blazer. Which is red, green and piss yellow. There are also huge black frame glasses that take up half his face. His hair is shaved on the sides. The top, however, is lavender and has been styled and gel'd as such that it looks like a swirl. Basically, a purple dog poop. He has a brown satchel bag slung over his shoulder. His very appearance hurts like a hangover.

His friend is not any better, shorter and rounder with long hair and full very bushy unkempt beard adorned with beads. He is wearing jeans with a torn black skirt over them, combat boots and a stained, Mickey Mouse sweatshirt. To pull the look all together he also sports a Christmas scarf and a puce fedora.

"I've been blogging about your art and its influence on modern society as we know it."

"Thank you, but I don't believe in gratification. I feel I've evolved above praise, there is no satisfaction except in the epiphany I receive when I think of new art."

"Oh yeah, of course, I understand completely." The fat one is clearly lying and truthfully, I don't think either of them understands what the other one is saying.

"I also blogged about this new guy whose music I'm really into, he's like Elvis Costello without sounding derivative."

"I'm so over derivative music."

"The Hipster," Buzzington narrates, "first appearing in this form in the nineties but not identified as such until much later in 09. We believe them to originate from Brooklyn but the true designation is not known. They are usually white millennials who occupy gentrified urban areas." Buzzington hands me a small black fanny pack and rushes the two as they pass an opening to an alley, I follow. He grabs the skinny one and I tackle the fat one in the same fashion. We push them into the alley like a couple of muggers.

The fat one puts up no fight and just lays there, shaking like a Chihuahua. The skinny one struggles against Buzzington, who is surprisingly strong. The skinny one's body flops up and down. He is letting out squeaks and squeals like a terrified marine animal pulled out of a net on the deck of a boat.

"They are defenseless against any attack that is not verbally based. As you can see the Hipster has virtually no upper body strength." Buzzington forces the skinny one down. He waves his hands wildly like a T-rex with down-syndrome as Buzzington coo's at him to try and calm him. "Derek the pack please," he says holding out his hand. I hand it over, the fat one is putting up no struggle whatsoever, but the smell emanating from him is awful. The Professor notices my face. "He must not use deodorant, believing it to be cancer-causing, possibly uses alternative methods like crystals or coconut oil." Buzzington pulls a tagging gun from his belt. I've seen the kind before when they tag sharks on Shark Week. The needle is very big.

I look down at the fat one, "Use deodorant you goddamn hippie. It's worth cancer if it means not going through life repelling everyone you ever meet. No wonder you can't get laid!"

"Aluminum is not meant to be used on the human body!" The fat one spits out in protest. I raise my balled fist up and he squeals loudly before fainting.

"I intend to study their mating habits, which can be tricky because for the most part they seem asexual or are constantly undecided between same and opposite-sex partners."

The skinny hipster looks like a helpless seal as Buzzington brings the tagging gun to his ear and punctures it through. A small green tag with the number seven on it now hangs from the bloody hipster's ear. Buzzington releases him and he scurries next to some trashcans, looking frightened. He paws at his ear, whimpering.

Buzzington comes over and tags the fat one too. Who on his back, looks like a badly dressed tortoise.

"These two will help me track and locate the mating grounds of this particular group of Hipsters. I had tremendous success with this approach in the late nineties with the Goths."

Buzzington finishes up and makes loud clicking noises until we have backed completely out of the alleyway. Then he motions for me to head back to the van. I watch as the skinny one rushes to the fat one, who is slowly coming to.

"They will pass off the tags as some other new fashion trend, or simply say they do not know or care when someone asks them about it. Their lack of commitment to even their own persons makes them so easy to study." Buzzington shakes my hand, "You have helped me enough for one night Derek and I appreciate it greatly."

"Thank you, Professor, I've learned quite a lot tonight. I hope your research goes well." I hand him back the fanny pack, but he refuses it.

"Just a couple of souvenirs for you take on your journey my new friend."

I move to the sidewalk. The hipsters have retreated back from the direction they were coming from when we stopped them. Buzzington gets back in the van. I am kind of sad to see him go. My curiosity alone to know what he is doing with all those specimens we collected would drive me to spend all night with him. If only life was like one of those *Choose Your Own Adventure* books. Then I could see how Buzzington would play out, then come back to this spot and go about my way. I always cheated at those damn books.

"Derek," he shouts out of the window as he pulls away, "you are by far the least annoying Millennial I've ever met until we meet again my friend." He waves goodbye.

"Good journey," I wave back as he pulls away and I watch the white van drive off into the night.

Swine should be just around the corner and I start walking only to stop at a crosswalk waiting for the little man to turn green. Standing next to me is a college-aged girl talking loudly into her cell phone. That in itself annoys me; no one else wants to hear your damn conversation. Her conversation is further bothersome. She uses words likes "totes", and her constant repetition of everyone being "Bae" is migraine-inducing. I look into the fanny pack and see salvation. The good professor left me a miniature version of his tranq gun and four darts.

"She's Bae, and you know this." The annoying girl continues.

Should I?

"OMG, he's Bae. Please, I can't even with you right now and I told my mother that she better be buying me a new car, I don't even care."

I should. And I do.

The dart sticks into her thigh and she turns and looks at me about to go off when her eyes roll back into her head and she falls to the sidewalk. Thankfully no one is around. I position her sitting on a bus stop bench a few feet away. Someone will undoubtedly think she's just a basic bitch who is passed out. Plus, that dart was small so it probably wears off quickly.

I walk across the street and make my way to the club. I probably shouldn't have done that, wasted one of those darts I mean. But it was fun, and you have to have a little fun in your life.

5: A Dirty Shame

How did I get here?

No seriously, I'm asking because I don't know when or where the night turned on me or how I ended up here.

Here being in the basement of the club Swine, strapped to a St. Andrews cross, half-naked, my legs held up by two muscular hairy men. I'm about to be penetrated by a ridiculously large black dildo that has been affectionately referred to as "Kunta Kinte." I really want to be offended by this, but honestly, the blatant racism is not high on my list of issues right now. There are more pressing matters, as in Kunta pressing against my no-no special place.

Maybe I should go back just a little.

It takes a few minutes of searching and asking a couple of random strangers, but I finally find the damn club. Its entrance isn't on the street, so you have to go around the side of the building and down an alley. Very sketchy, like I could get hepatitis just from the railing kind of sketchy. The alley is bathed in a soft red glow illuminating from the large neon sign shaped like a pig above the door touting the club's name - Swine. No fancy entrance, no bouncer or long line of people waiting to get inside. I go up to the door and reach out for the handle when the slot slides open and two intense blue eyes stare out at me.

"Password?"

What the fuck? Seriously? No one said anything about a damn password. Why didn't I Goggle the club's website, or check it out on Facebook or Twitter? Jesus Christ, I'm fucking slacking tonight. The eyes keep staring at me so I blurt out the first thing I can think of.

"Fidelio"

The slot slams close and the door opens. The club is very dark, bathed much like the alleyway, in a soft red glow. It is coming from red lights tucked in floor and ceilings against the black painted walls. The main entryway is an open space. To the left, I can see the bar and the little lounge area around it with old ratty beat-up couches and mismatched loveseats. A few guys looking pretty haggard, most likely at the end of their high, are mingling around having some drinks. To the right is a small dance floor. A few "disco" lights, clearly bought from Spencer's Gifts are in the ceiling. A small DJ booth is nestled against the back wall. The DJ is a handsome guy bouncing his head along to the beat. This makes up a small portion of the club, a little off-centered in the middle is a hallway and I know instantly exactly what kind of club, Swine is.

Yes, there are clubs to dance all night away in Donna Summer style. Bars for drinking all night long with your friends. Then there are places like Swine, where you go to have a drink and get off. You can hear the faint moans and groans of pleasure over the loud music. I resist my urge to go wander and play, I'm no prude and it's been a long night after all, but I have a goal though and I just want to bring this night to a close.

And get back to my couch. That beautiful bastard that I know misses me as much as I miss it.

I head to the left. A couple of guys are lingering around the bar, beers, and cigarettes in their hands. Their eyes are constantly scanning the crowd, looking for their next playmate. An older guy, slightly handsome with salt and pepper hair gives me a look and smiles. I don't smile back. Non-verbal communication is king in this kind of place, and a smile might be misconstrued as the acceptance of an invitation to meet in a dark corner and bang.

I lean up against the bar, and an exhausted looking older woman comes over. She is clearly unhappy with the choices she's made in her life. She scowls at me and demands to know what I'm having. I order a shot of Silver Patron and slide my card over the bar to her. She huffs when I tell her to close it out. What? Does she get paid per bar tab or something? I can't do bar tabs. The minute I hand over my card and start ordering drinks I forget about how much actual money I have and start rolling like a Rockefeller. Then under the haze of a hangover, I see what I paid in the morning and almost pass out. Especially with no one I know here to reel me in. I'll stick to paying per drink, thank you very much Hagatha.

She slams the Patron in front of me. I tip her graciously – three bucks for one-shot should earn me some points.

It doesn't.

"I'm looking for someone," I ask her as she takes my signed receipt.

"So is everyone in here," her raspy, I've smoked three packs a day voice tells me. "You think you're special?"

"Well yes, yes I do, my mommy tells me so every day. I need to find someone named Bull the Null."

She steps back and looks me over, "You're not his type princess sparkle."

Well, clearly I and this fucking hag are not meant to be the best of friends. "First off, I'm everyone's type okay. I'm fucking adorable. Secondly, I'm looking to acquire something from him, not fuck. So if you're done judging Judy, can you tell me where he is and then get me another shot?" I slide the empty shot glass across the bar to her.

She snaps it up and pours the tequila, sliding it back to me. "On the house, and sure, I'll tell him an adorable fag in a He-Man shit is looking for him. He's probably busy so it might be a while."

Sarcastic bitch, it's really all I can to not tranq dart her ass right now. "You do that Cuntzilla. I'll be around." I think she growls at me but I knock my shot back and turn around. Hagatha moves to the far end of the bar and picks up a phone.

I head out and move toward the dance floor to get another glance at the cute DJ. This area of the club is virtually empty. Except for a trio of hairy gay men are living it up on the dancefloor to Lady GaGa's Just Dance. Very touchy-feely with each other which in a place like this where ass and cock are running around like free-range chicken means they are on ecstasy or 'Molly' as the kids call it today.

I look past the touchy-feely trio and into the DJ booth. With his dark brown hair, fair skin with a little scruff on his face, and gorgeous dark eyes. The DJ is known as Joey Watts. He's very handsome and the newest possible candidate in the running to be my very own future ex-husband.

I move along the edge of the dance floor to get a little closer, maybe I can kill some time before Bull the Null and strike up a conversation. It's not like anyone in this place is listening to the music. In the few feet it takes to get me closer I've already imagined everything about this guy. Firstly, he likes all the same movies I like. He's ready to settle down with me, move to the country, and adopt a baby from some inner-city crack whore. Do they even still call them crack babies or is that not P.C anymore? I can see our Christmas cards now, everyone in matching sweaters. We're the envy of all the other couples. We will be so...on second thought, As I peer further into the booth my mind is changed. He is bent over his turntables with his pants down around his ankles. His Nintendo controller shaped belt buckle is smacking against the concrete floor and behind him standing at only 4 feet high is a blond-haired midget - or is it little person? Short person? Tiny dancer? Dwarf seems very wrong unless we're in Middle Earth. Listen, I seriously don't fucking know. He's a shorty and he is dressed in a black robe, which I instantly recognize as Hogwarts standard issue. He's wearing the yellow Hufflepuff house scarf around his neck and in the back pocket, I see a wand. I realize quickly it is actually a dildo; a dildo shaped like Harry Potter's wand. His right arm is oddly muscular compared to the rest of his body and far larger than it should be. Almost cartoonish especially considering it is in the middle of fisting DJ Joey Watts ass. Not just casual friendly fisting either. He is really rooter-rooting that ass. So much vigor, such enthusiasm, oh Jesus he is elbow deep in it! Any deeper and he could probably operate Joey Watts like a damn puppet.

"Fistorium Incantatem!" I hear the guy shout in a tiny high pitched voice, as he retracts his arm then shoves it back in.

Joey Watts moans loudly, "get it Dobby! Get it!"

The tiny tot does indeed get fast and furious on that ass.

"Fist my Goblet of Fire. Yes! Yes! Raid my Azkaban, RAID IT." Joey Watts demands, crying out in ecstasy as he looks over and shoots me a smile and a wink.

Jesus fucking Christ.

I stood wide-eyed and speechless, I mean what does one say in this situation anyway; '*I like your technique*'? I turn my attention quickly away and look past the trio of Bears dancing, faking like I see my friends that I wave wildly too and walk quickly away.

I go back to the bar and order a Heineken from Cunty McGee, who I am very certain snarls at me this time. It appears it is still going to be a while before this Bull guy graces me with his presence. As I wait for her to bring me my beer, which I'm certain she would piss in if she had a dick and could do so, the older guy with the salt and pepper hair comes over and leans against the bar next to me.

"They say you can feel it in your stomach." He takes a drag on his cigarette as he grabs at his crotch through his Brooks Brothers suit.

What the fuck is happening in my life right now? "Just what every boy wants to hear." I quickly focus my attention away from him.

"I can be your Daddy." He adds with all seriousness like that would be a turn on.

"Well, then you need to go to the other side of the room and be cold and distant to me." I roll my eyes, grab my newly placed beer and walk away. "Be sure to tell anyone within earshot how much I've disappointed both you and Mom."

I should just go sit on one of the couches, which have filled up with men who are taking a rest from their activities. Some are drenched in sweat guzzling down water, other sipping beers or mixed drinks. My phone is at barely twenty percent, so how long can I stare at it before it just dies. Plus who knows what's next, I need to preserve the last juice in it for the Uber ride home. That leaves only the awful possibility of potentially interacting with the others sitting there. That is the very last thing I want to do.

I head toward the hall and into the heart of the club. Ahead of me is laid out like a cheaply made haunted house maze. The hallways lead to small alcoves, private rooms, and around one bend is a small theatre. There are no chairs, only carpeted cover risers for sitting on. They are showing some delightful vintage porn. A few guys are resting in there, hands firmly on their exposed cocks. I find it hard to jerk off to the porn from yesteryear as I realize most of those guys are probably dead now. I personally find it difficult to keep up an erection to dead people. These guys are not having any problem though. I stand in the entryway for a couple of minutes and watch the men in the audience. How they nervously eyeball each other, some scooting closer to others. Slowly, of course, no sudden movements, you'll scare the closeted straight men.

I sip my beer and move on. I walk past a row of men all facing a wall. Takes me a minute to realize it is a wall of glory holes. Yep, on the other side, in individual rooms are eager gentlemen. Judging from the moaning, they are taking very good care of business.

Past the glory hole hollow is a small room with two sex swings hanging in it. In one is a skinny guy dressed all in black latex, a hood completely covering his face. Nothing creeps me out more than the dehumanization aspect of a lot of the kinkier sex fetishes. I once dated, briefly, a guy named Bruce. Bruce was a big burly construction worker by day. By night, he liked to be on a leash and treated literally like a dog. In his apartment he had a dog bowl he would eat out of on the floor. Sex with him was very weird, and I only did it once, okay twice, fine four, maybe five times max. Six times, but after he asked me to take him for a walk in public and I said enough was enough and only fucked once more.

Latex boy is in the swing, and several men are taking turns fucking him. He can't see anything as his eyes are covered, and I don't think he can hear in that hood either. In the creepiest aspect of it, the mouth hole is sewn shut. Poor due can't even blurt out his safe word.

The other side of the room, a handsome, also fairly thin guy, with both arms completely tattooed, is bound up by ropes and suspended from the ceiling. Another group of men is tormenting him by not allowing him to come. He begs and pleads, but they deny him.

I spot two guys staring at me, their attention no longer on the trussed-up, bound guy. One guy looks in his fifties, overly tanned, bleach hair and wearing only a tiny gold speedo. His body used to be muscular and taut but now it is sagging with age. I'm pretty sure he still sees himself as twenty-two when he looks in the mirror. You do you Boo.

Standing next to him and also staring me down like I'm the next meal on the buffet is a very large, African-American gentleman wearing only a pair of gray track pants and some Timberlands. I love track pants, especially when guys wear them with no underwear. Nothing I love more in life than a visible penis line. Sweatpants are to gay guys what yoga pants are too straight men. This guy is very noticeable, but really I consider everyone else second rate after seeing RJ.

Just like that, my mind wanders off thinking of that gorgeously insane college boy. It is his penis I'm thinking about when the weird man grabs my arm and catches me off guard I seriously didn't even see him coming.

"I must paint you" he declares triumphantly.

Oh, fuck not this again. No seriously, ever since the nineties people are always telling me they want to paint me. I don't consider myself portrait material mind you, but this is like the fifth offer in these many years. So maybe I'm born with it, who knows?

"I use my penis as the brush" He shakes his hips smiling at me like a deranged preschooler ready to finger-paint on a rainy afternoon.

I look down and see his penis has been released from the gold speedo. The poor little thing, it looks so fatigued. Like a sad, paint-covered retail worker forced to do overtime with no lunch break.

"You paint with your dick for real?"

He nods enthusiastically. I always did want a portrait of myself, hanging in the living room, very old school Playboy bachelor style. At least this one would come with an interesting backstory. 'Why yes," I would tell my guests, 'the gentleman used his genitalia' and we would laugh and laugh.

"I want to do still life now though not just portraits - so my vision is for you to lie down, while Big Black Maurice takes a dump on your chest."

And I'm out.

I look over and see Big Black Maurice nodding, licking his lips and rubbing his stomach.

I haven't moved that fast away from someone since the time I sharted my pants in line at Quiznos. Don't judge me, we have all gambled on a fart and lost that bet, besides I was in a Quiznos, not like anyone could tell anyway.

As I meander through the halls, guys grab my arms, trying to pull me toward them. More of that non-verbal communication I was talking about. A grab means they are interested in you. I'm surprised by the attention I seem to be generating. This is how the gay universe works. If this was any other night when I wanted to get laid by a dozen strangers I doubt anyone would be talking to me.

One guy, around my age, pulls me to him and tells me all he wants to do is 'hibernate inside my asshole until winter is over.'

Ya know some guys just say the sweetest things.

The two shots and now finished beer have made their presence to my bladder known. I move through the handsy crowd; my ass is getting groped, my front is getting groped, now I'm not complaining mind you, but I'm on a mission tonight. I see a sign pointing to the bathroom when I'm stopped yet again. This time I mean older, older like could be a great-great-grandfather old. He succeeds in pinning me against the wall and runs his skeletal fingers over my lips. I gag at the smell of days old Ben-Gay.

"I like you," his hisses in a gravelly voice.

"Um, thank you?" I try to move but he puts up his hand blocking me.

"Cute thing like you shouldn't be walking around here alone."

I'll take 'Things a rapist will say for five hundred Alex'.

He gets his face closer to mine. It's a face out of a nightmare. Sunken cheeks, pale skin, and dark receded eyes. He's terrifying. I am certain this is the evil preacher from *Poltergeist II* come to life and is ready to start singing to me at any moment, "*God is in his holy temple.*"

"Man I gotta piss okay, and seriously not interested." I don't know why I'm trying to be so polite about this.

"You can piss in my mouth."

For fuck sakes.

"I'll be your own personal toilet."

"There are a couple of guys over there looking for someone to take a shit on. You guys could be real forever friends."

"I want your young cum."

Fuck me, this is how I die. He's going to wear my skin around his house like a robe while he watches daytime television. "Listen, Crypt Keeper, I'm done, I already said I'm not interested. And frankly, I don't think you should even be attempting such vigorous sexual activity at your age anyway. You're dried up like a piece of balsa wood and the friction could start a fire, and I only practice safe sex."

"No need to be an asshole Mary!" he snaps.

'*Mary*' for you kids following along at home, is an antiquated colloquialism used by homosexuals in the seventies and eighties. They would call each other it, or heterosexuals would use it in a more negative connotation. It is still used in some places today. Obviously, Gramps here has not updated his lingo for the new millennium. I laugh it off because it is hysterical. "And like do you even ejaculate or is it just the condensed powder version now?" I push his decrepit hand off me. He gives up and turns and off in search of new prey. Thank goodness too. I did not want to waste a tranq dart on his scrawny old man ass. It could probably kill him and I don't need that on my conscience, not with everything else.

I turn the corner and go off to find the bathroom. When I do, sheer dread hits me the moment I enter: it's a trough. Dammit, nothing I hate more than trough peeing. Why can't they have urinals or stalls? I am slightly pee shy. Sure drinking helps to overcome it, but I've not drunk nearly enough tonight. And the real issue comes when I saddle up to said urinal and then am unable to go, so there I stand with my junk in my hand not going, looking like some sick creeper only there to peep other dicks.

It's why I love the privacy of a stall, it still takes me a minute to go but there is no pressure. No such luck tonight though. This tiny bathroom is just two sinks and a trough that takes up one whole wall. There are a few men going when I finally step up to it and find a spot between them. The process takes all my concentration. Finally after what is most likely only thirty seconds, but feels much longer, my stream starts and I feel the instant relief.

I feel some wetness on the cuff of my jeans at the bottom of my right leg. I check myself. My stream is straight and true. I look to my right and see a nice looking guy in his mid-forties, thick beard, bright eyes, wearing only a leather harness across his chest. He's turned in my direction, lightly pissing on my leg. He has a big smile on his face and says he is pissing on me to show me how much he likes me.

I seriously just want to go home.

"No," is all I can muster as I shake off my junk, tuck it back in my jeans and quickly leave the bathroom. I am done with this place. I am all for everyone to do what they want to do. Fuck how they want to fuck, but this whole place is a bit much for me right now. I start to make my way for the front, fuck the weed, fuck getting pissed on. I am so done. Someone grabs my arm again. I turn to shout but am cut off. The guy is a little younger than me, tall and wiry with short black hair and blue eyes hidden under a very bushy Unibrow. His black leather pants are so tight I'm not sure how blood is even flowing to his legs and he's shirtless.

"Follow me, Bull will see you now."

I follow him to a door marked 'Private', he nods to the large bouncer guarding it, who nods back and opens the door. There is a staircase that leads us to the basement.

The entire basement is a literal sex dungeon. It is as big as the club above, set up in similar maze style but the walls are done in faux stone like a castle's dungeon. There's no music down here so the sounds of sex and various other activities are clearer. Unibrow leads me around until we come to a rather large room with a St. Andrews cross against one wall. On the opposite wall various toys, gags, paddles and the lot arranged nicely on shelves.

"I'm not here to fuck or be fucked, I told the hag in the black leather jacket that earlier. I am here to see Bull the Null about buying some weed."

Unibrow doesn't answer, he motions for me to go across the room, which I do. "Remove your pants."

"I think you have the wrong idea about me, and apparently about eyebrows. There should be two." I point to his head. "I just wanna buy some pot from this Bull guy and be on my way. I've had a very long night and -" I am cut off by the cracking of a whip. Instantly my ass cheeks clench. Where'd he pull a whip from? "Simmer down Catwoman, I just told you I'm not into this shit."

"Take off your pants." Unibrow commands, "or we'll do it for you." Two large, muscular hairy men, nearly naked except for small black speedos come out from behind Unibrow as if hearing their cue and start heading toward me.

I put my hands quickly behind my back and scoot the pack Buzzington had given me up my torso further. Hoping it won't be discovered. I get it up and out of the way, just as BeeBop and Rocksteady grab me and pull off my jeans. My underwear goes along with them. Wonderful. They go for my shirt but I protest, "Please I have body image issues, can we leave the shirt on?"

"Fine," Unibrow motions toward the cross with his head and BeeBop and Rocksteady gingerly lift me up and strap my wrists into the cuffs on the top of the cross.

What kind of fucked-up Fifty Shades of Rainbow ass nonsense am I going to have to deal with now?

He walks over to the wall of toys and pulls down a very ridiculously large veiny black dildo. BeeBop and Rocksteady pull my legs up. I am more worried about the fanny pack being discovered than the anal torture Kunta is about to deliver to me. The cuff around my left wrist is not secured all the way and I can wiggle my hand out but I don't do it just yet. I'm no action movie star. There's no way I can do some impressive series of moves where with one hand I retrieve the tranq gun, kick BeeBop and Rocksteady in the face, tranq the hell out of Unibrow and escape. I'm no Jason Bourne, but really neither is Jeremy Renner for that matter. That movie – sheesh, what were they thinking.

Unibrow pushes Kunta between my cheeks and starts a knock-knock knocking on heaven's door.

"I do not consent," I say wiggling my ass away from him when I see a man enter the room from over Unibrow's head. He coughs upon his entrance and Unibrow jumps back. My ass sighs with relief as he takes Kunta with him. The man is obviously Bull the Null, and he is in his late forties. He's a good six feet, a mix of somewhat muscular and somewhat chubby, a genre of man I've always liked. Very tan and with a full grey beard and he is smiling brightly as he enters. His face looks kind. And he's wearing a hunter green crushed velour robe tied loosely around his waist. I can see tuffs of grey chest hair peeking out from the top. He doesn't speak right away but he clearly is commanding this room. Unibrow walks over to him, head down like he's misbehaved. Which I would believe was a good thing in this place. He chastises Unibrow with his intense eyes and waves his hands, a silent command for BeeBop and Rocksteady to release my legs. They do and move away, stepping around behind him. I'm still strapped to the cross, well, as far as they know, when Bull steps closer to me. "I am the ultimate bottom!" He declares to all who are listening and throws open his robe in a dramatic gesture usually reserved for drag queens.

He is a very masculine sight. His large chest is covered in hair and not going to lie I am slightly attracted as my eyes survey his large body. Well, that is until I see his crotch. If there was a record playing it would have scratched to a stop. His crotch is completely devoid of anything. Yep, you heard me right, no dick, no balls, nada. There is a small hole where the base of his penis used to be buried in a sizeable bush of pubic hair.

What in fresh fucking fuckery fuck is going on in this place?

"Behold my null and void!" He runs his hands down along his non-existent privates and then his head shoots up and looks directly into my eyes. "I hear you were looking for me?"

"Uh yeah, RJ sent me. He said I could get some pot from you. You obviously have other things going on though, so I'll just go."

"Why leave us so soon, I am still all that is a man." He runs his hand along my chest.

"I am not doubting that."

"You think I want to be a woman?" He snatches his hand away as if offended, "well I don't, that's not what this is about." He's defensive despite my lack of response. "I was never happy, even as a teen *it* made me upset. This," he rubs his void again, "this was my way to freedom!"

"But dude, your dick, c'mon." I know I shouldn't interact with the crazy, but I can't help it. I like dick. I am a big fan of dick, like the number one fan. I'd lock it in a cabin and force it to write me a novel type of number one fan.

"I am a bottom!" He yells. "My cock was never for me. It was always someone else's. Their tool and it meant nothing to me, NOTHING. I would vomit when I topped. The very idea of using that appendage to please someone else instead of using my own hole sickened me." He walks around the room while he talks. The other three stand back quietly just observing. "The men love it you know," his voice no longer anger-filled, now bordering on somewhat seductive. "No pesky penis to get in the way. Just them, my hole, and absolute pleasure. I let them lay me down, we can be face to face while they fuck me with no awkward cock in the way. I can wet their stomach with my juices."

Juices? Did he seriously just say he has juices?

I've died, that's what happened, somewhere along the course of tonight I died and I just don't realize it yet. I am stuck in some kind of fucked-up purgatory for all eternity with this 'Null' dude and a rabid female sea manatee that want to fuck me. I should have probably been nicer to people or something, I guess? I'm so sorry baby Jesus.

"I can see the questions in your face. Your curious when most people are so ignorant. They think everything comes from the testicles, but my juices originate in the seminal vesicles and the prostate, only the baby-making ingredient comes from the testis. I still come." He shouted, very proud of the last statement.

"I am very happy for you and your life choices. Do you have any pot or not?"

"I ate my own testicles once they were cut." He says slightly dazed and I don't feel like he is even addressing me anymore. He's riding a wave of nostalgia to the beach on Fucked-Up Island. "I used a simple recipe; some butter with a few fresh Portobello mushrooms. Paired it with a nice red, a nice seventy-three. One from the collection my bastard father had left me."

If I am not already dead, I'd really like to be right now.

"They were quite good, tasted slightly like chicken."

Jesus, take the wheel 'cause I can't even.

Bull pulls an item off of the shelf housing all the toys, a cylinder case covered by a black cloth. "I couldn't eat this though," he removes the cover.

Yep, it's his dick, nicely preserved in a glass jar. It looks rather large which makes its removal all the sadder.

"Bull, the pot?" I ask wearily.

"I'm afraid I am all out at the moment. I only have my personal stash, but that's unimportant."

"Um, it is important, it is literally the only reason I am here right now."

"You're very attractive." He eyes me intently.

Not this again, well at least he too has a cunt I can kick if need be.

BeeBop and Rocksteady remove their speedos revealing they too are Nulls. Unibrow is as well, though I can't really tell because his pubic bush is out of control. I am certain there are some Cub Scouts camping in that mess somewhere earning their wilderness badges.

"Kunta was a test you see," Bull explains placing the pickled penis jar back on the shelf. "You did not welcome him with open ass. You are the special top we've been waiting for."

"Whoa now, just because I didn't want to be plowed like a field in Italy doesn't mean I am anything special. I'm just a delicate homosexual who relishes the ability to control his sphincter."

"You are the Ultimate Top, and you have come to fuck us."

Beebop, Rocksteady, and Unibrow all assume their positions on the floor. On their hands and knees with their asses pointed up at me.

"Wait, are you telling me that every other guy you have brought down here took Kunta?"

He nods.

"All of them? Seriously that thing's circumference is like, you know what, never mind that's not important right now. Bull, I am all for everyone getting freaky however they want to get freaky. But this scene is not for me."

Bull moves quickly and stands right in front of me. He begins undoing the straps around my wrists. His null and voided area rubs against my crotch. My poor defenseless exposed crotch, and yeah I can feel those juices. I gag, but keep it quiet. I don't want the crazy man to stop untying me.

"You are the top we've been waiting for, fill our holes and help make our juices flow." Bull joins the others on the floor. They begin to chant in unison for me to release their juices. I can see their hands rubbing their voids in excitement. They wave their hairy asses in the air begging for me to come to enter. I feel it coming and there's no stopping it. Nope, nothing I can do can stifle the...

I projectile vomit.

Yes, an epic tsunami of vomit catapults its way out of my throat and showers them. I'm not even finished heaving as I make my move and grab my pants pulling them on. I wipe the vomit off my mouth and quickly look around. I see my beacon of hope. A bright red EXIT sign only a few feet away but they are in my way along with a hell of a lot of puke.

"FUCK US," Bull yells at me. He flings himself onto his back and throws his legs into the air. "I am the ultimate bottom, come find solace in me."

The vomit has not deterred them. They're fucking writhing in it. Beebop and Rocksteady have begun to make out and when I look Unibrow appears to be giving their voided areas oral sex. Bull's eyes are locked on me, he demands I pleasure him. I reach up under my shirt and pull the pack down. I don't even aim the tranq gun. I just fire blindly and somehow the dart finds its way right into Bull's sweet spot.

"My urethra," he shouts as his eyes cross and he passes out. I do not hesitate another minute. I rush past them to the emergency exit door. It leads to some stairs which I follow then finally I am out into the sweet air of freedom. I look behind me and see Beebop and Rocksteady charging after me. Unibrow is behind them demanding they bring me back to pay for what I've done. That's me making friends everywhere I go. I race down the alley and toward the street.

A silver car pulls up onto the curb and begins to honk repeatedly until I look at it. It is DJ Joey Watts behind the wheel. "Get in!" he shouts as I make a beeline for the passenger side door. I slam it shut and he speeds off before I can be apprehended.

6. Polyester

DJ Joey Watts slows down after only getting half a block away. Three naked guys with no dicks, covered in vomit aren't going to be chasing anyone more than a few feet.

I click my seatbelt as I look around his messy little sedan. The radio isn't playing which I find odd until he strangely seems to read my mind. "Sorry, this is my free time from the music. I need quiet after my sets."

Apart from our breathing, there is no noise for a good five minutes. "Thank you for that." I finally blurt out.

"No problem. Those guys are a bit intense. It's from all the testosterone shots they have to take. You know since they have no balls." He says it so straightforwardly I can't help but laugh aloud a little. "When I did my first audition for the DJ gig I had to take their ultimate top test. I didn't pass."

It is not hard to believe witnessing the fisting action from earlier. I look down at his seat and see he is sitting on a small red inflatable donut. I resist the urge to giggle. Etiquette states one shouldn't mock someone who's rescued them. I check my phone. As feared it's completely dark now. The battery drained. My connection to the outside world is dead and gone.

I am so done with this night.

"Look, thanks again for rescuing me. You're my knight in shining whatever model this car is, but just drop me off at the nearest subway station or street that has some bars on it. I will hail a cab and call it a night."

"Oh," he looks surprised. "I thought you wanted some herb? Sorry but I overheard. I came down to the dungeon a little after you to get some more lube for Dobby. I saw them stripping your pants off and strapping you up. Dobby texted right then that he thought his wrist was dislocated and he was leaving for the ER. They have such brittle bones ya know, hollow like a bird. So I figured if he was done then I'd just stay and jerk off to the show. That's when it seemed to get out of hand. I ran out to grab my car and figure a way to help you get out of there."

"You don't even know me though."

"I know, but I saw you earlier and you seemed cute and nice. I figured what the hell. Anyway, I know this lady, she's an English teacher but sells weed on the side to supplement her income. We really don't pay educators enough. Good shit too. I figured I'd just take you out to her place in the burbs."

"Wait, like the suburbs?" I look out the window and see we're nearing Fifty-Six; one of the several freeways that lead out of the city. I don't normally see this view except on an early Sunday morning with Craig and Andy. I am usually still half asleep or hungover in the back of the car.

"Yeah, once we hit the freeway it's only like a five-minute drive to her place. We can swing by, get you what you need and then head back in. I can take you back to your car or home if you'd like."

This is too good to be true, which for this night means it probably is. "Please don't take this the wrong way, but I've had a real cluster fuck of a night. So I'm just gonna come right out and ask – what is that you want from me for doing all of this?"

Joey looks a little taken aback and I instantly feel like an asshole. "I, um, nothing, I was thinking about getting some for myself. Figured I'd be nice and help you out."

Fuck, he's a sweet guy and I need to relax. Granted this night has given me the right to be uptight and cautious. I need to be able to see a friendly gesture for what it is, just a friendly gesture.

"And you have really nice hands, so maybe you could take over where Dobby left off?"

There it is.

"Only if you would want to of course, if not it's okay. I got toys at home."

Seriously dude? How much more can his poor asshole take? I kinda want to call someone about it. Surely there is some group to report the inhumane way this guy treats his sphincter. I decline politely. Fistings have never really been my kind of thing. He looks a little disappointed, but we press on to the freeway.

At Twelve fifty-five at night the freeway is nearly dead. Joey goes on about being a DJ, loving music, the beat, the drop or whatever. I don't know any of the musical terms he is throwing around. Plus I am not really paying attention. With my head against the window, I watch the city lights, my apartment, my bed, the cute psychotic soon to be ex-boyfriend RJ. I watch it all get further away. This sudden stop in the momentum of the evening starts to let a lot of things sink in.

I am tired. I've been up since six a.m. remember. That I can deal with. Undoubtedly a second wind will kick up in me at any time. I'm no pansy. Once an evening starts I can usually rock it out till three or four a.m. often I am the last man standing. This evening is different though. I've had two different rounds of drinks with a large time in between. Their collective buzzes have worn off. That in itself always makes me feel weird. My body isn't sure if it's drunk, going to get drunk or if it needs to start the process of the hangover. My body is kinda a dick and it can't just go back to being normal. No that'd be too fucking easy.

More importantly though and most crucial, I am starving. I had not realized how hungry I was until right now. Especially seeing how I had left the entirety of my stomach contents in a gross mess on the floor in Swine. I had not eaten anything since I went home to change and head out to start this night. Imperial Chinese's amazing pork fried rice and eggrolls are just a cruel unrealized dream now.

I'm tired and hungry and despite the promise of the drugs, I just want to be home. I want to be in my bed or on my couch. No offense to the talkative cutie next to me but I am so not in the mood for his take on how music is the key to everlasting life. I turn and look at him every few minutes and realize how cute he is. Then he shifts on the donut and it lets out a small squeak. Cute or not it takes everything I have to not let out hysterical laughter.

We cross the drawbridge over the canal and I know just a couple more miles and we are fully in the burbs. Identical houses, strip malls, and of course housewives. Those housewives according to television are either desperate or "real". Sorry but I am a city guy. The suburbs or the rural country life that lies past it just does not appeal to me. I need bustling streets, rude people, and food places that deliver any hour. Food, fucking hell I'd slap my momma for some food. I think about maybe asking him if he has anything. Judging from my filthy surroundings, however, I decide not to. His car

is a collection of old greases stained take out bags, gym
clothes and cd cases strewn everywhere. I was lucky he
had a piece of gum, which did nothing for my vomit
mouth. Surely some fast food joint around here has to be
twenty-four hours. A greasy triple cheeseburger right
now would be heavenly.

Joey Watts takes the second exit and right on cue
a moment later there is a strip mall complete with an
Applebee's. Joey knows where he is going and navigates
the side roads until we come upon a picturesque tree-
lined street with cute houses all lined up in rows. The
houses were not identical however so I feel cheated and
lied to by the media's portrayal of the suburbs. Each one
is charming in its own way. Joey pulls over to the right
and stops against the curb putting the car in park. "We
need to park a bit away, not trying to make her spot hot."

I follow him down the sidewalk. He is bopping
his head to music only he can hear. It is so very quiet
here. I can hear some crickets and the soothing hoot of an
owl. It's like I'm in a fucking nature movie. No sirens, no
people yelling. How the hell does anyone get any sleep
around here? Joey stops and points over to the right. At
the end of the block on the corner is a quaint little single-
family starter home painted bright yellow.

It's idyllic with a small white picket fence around
it. There are big windows in the front and a dainty porch
with some plants hanging from the eaves in terracotta
pots. One look and I know instantly that it behind the
door, hanging on those walls are the single worst pieces
of décor in existence. Bossy Signs! Oh, you know what
I'm talking about. Those stupid wooden art pieces you
can find at Michael's or Home Goods. Well anywhere
really that sells home décor. They are the kind of signs
that demand you "Live Laugh Love" or "Never Stop
Dreaming." Is there anything fucking worse than going to
someone's house and being bossed around by tiny, or

sometimes large, plaques hanging on the walls? Maybe I don't want to fucking "Live Every Moment to the Fullest." I went to a baby shower once for a stupid friend who was already three fucking kids deep. In the bathroom there was a sign telling me to "Brush, Floss, Flush." Seriously? Assholes.

We make our way up the drive but we go past the front porch and head around to the side. There's a short four-step staircase leading to the basement door. The light is on above it. I look past the back of the house and see a small alley between this house and the one behind it. Parked in it is a brown van, a dark brown seventies-era conversion van. I know it's the same one I saw when driving around with Buzzington.

"Lights on means she's doing business." Joey starts down the stairs but stops and turns to me. "I've never come this late before and never unannounced so I don't know what is going to happen."

I slap his arm with a sense of familiarity like we've been friends for twenty years. "You didn't text or call her first?" I chastise him. "What the hell is wrong with you?"

He shrugs and goes to the door. He raises his hand to knock but the door flies inward before he can. A hand brandishing a large butcher knife starts swinging in our face. A feminine voice demands we come in quickly.

Beyond the door is a small square unfinished laundry room. We enter and the door slams close behind us. The only light is coming from the open door on the opposite end of the tight quarters. Holding the knife is a tall, lanky woman with brownish-grey hair that hangs down to her bottom but is held up in a bun. Several strands have escaped their prison and hang wildly in her face. Two piercing hazel eyes glare out from behind a pair of small round glasses. She's homely looking, and her clothes aren't doing much for her either. She is clearly frazzled. Her skin is wet with perspiration.

"And what pray tell are you two doing sneaking around my house at one in the morning?"

"Mrs. B, it's me, Joey Watts."

She looks at him closer and nods with recognition. She's apparently in the middle of something. Her attention keeps being pulled to whatever is behind the open door. "Oh yeah, I remember you, the queer Disc Jockey. What's up with this fag?" She points the knife in my face.

"Madam, if you please!" I feign offense to her comment, "I am a delicate homosexual."

She looks at me then lowers the knife. "I left the light on by accident. It's good you two happened upon my house tonight though. I need some more witnesses." Mrs. B doesn't say anything else and motions for us to follow her through the opposite door.

"Mrs. B," I say quietly, "we are here about the drugs."

"Call them pharmaceuticals, it's more gentile."

She says walking us through the door and into another small hallway with a staircase leading up into the house on the far end. To the right was a step down into her basement. She turned right.

Mrs. B pushes the door to her basement open and it is chaos, pure and utter chaos. The basement is set up like a courtroom. Straight ahead of me to my right against the wall is her honor's Judge's bench. To the right of that a projector screen is pulled down, glaring blinding white at the moment. It looked like a deranged version of that old show Night Court. Oh, Markie Post whatever happened to her?

To the left of me is a wall with a door leading to another room. The door is shut but lined up on either side of it are four people, all with their hands' zip-tied behind their back. Silver duct tape stretched across their mouths. Their eyes meet mine as I pass by them and silently plead with me for help. A very large black man with bulging arm muscles and no visible neck stands in the middle of them dressed as a bailiff. His face stoic and his arms folded across his chest. His eyes met also meet mine and say 'keep fucking moving.' There are sounds coming from the small room but I can't make out what they are. Though my gut tells me they are screams. Once again my night has taken the off-ramp into Whatthefuckville.

Past that mystery room is a pair of waist-high half walls, separated in the middle. Beyond those are rows of chairs. Mrs. B motions for us to go sit as she heads to her bench. Joey swings into the first chair in the first row. I sit next to him. Safer to have someone around to throw in the way in case shit gets crazy. He can be my distraction if I need to get the tranq gun. I kind of feel bad about using him as a potential human shield, but who knows what fuckery he has gotten me into.

A couple of seats behind us are two men. They're not sitting close to each other and both are wearing expensive suits. To the left of me across the aisle is an older woman. She's white-haired wearing a sensible cardigan and clutching her Coach knockoff for dear life. Were they here to buy weed too and just got caught up in all of, whatever, this is?

I turn my attention back to the front of the court. Right in front of the half walls and facing the bench is a table with two chairs. One of them occupied by a very frazzled looking overweight bald attorney. He is slumped over and frantically going through paperwork. There is a complete air of seriousness around all of this.

I lean over and whisper in Joey's ear, "What the hell is all of this?"

He shrugs. There is seriously nothing worse than a vapid non-responsive shrug as an answer. I want to hit him until he is dead.

"I've only ever been to the laundry room."

From the far side of the bench, another almost identical huge black bailiff steps forward. Did she put out a Craigslist ad for them? *Wanted imposing African-American males to keep order in a kangaroo court I conduct in my basement. No necks required.*

Where did they get the uniforms? Did she pay for the dry-cleaning? I have so many questions that I know I am never going to get the answers to.

"All rise, the honorable Judge B has declared court is back in session."

All of us in the audience stand up.

"Please be seated." Mrs. B addresses the court calmly, "Bailiff next case please."

"The People vs. Lina Tran."

I cannot see around the wall but I can hear the shuffle and the muffled protest. The other bailiff brings a twenty-something Asian girl over and sits her at the desk, snatching off the duct tape and cutting the zip tie before returning to his post.

"Miss Tran, do you know why you've been brought before this court?"

"I don't know who the fuck you are lady."

I watch as the bald guy next to her shakes his head.

Mrs. B slams her gavel down hard. "You will watch your mouth or you will be held in contempt." She goes from calm demeanor to full frenzied anger in like twelve seconds and her eyes are wild.

"Your honor," the bald guy finally speaks up, standing as he does. "My client was briefed prior to the recess, she is aware. It won't happen again."

"Thank you, Calvin. Now Miss. Tran, I'll repeat, do you know understand why you've been brought before the court tonight?"

"I really don't," Lina responds with that flippant tone all young people seem to have. They're so good at saying 'fuck you' without actually saying it.

Mrs. B purses her lips and smirks. "Is this your Facebook page?" Mrs. B points to the screen on the wall which now projects an image of Lina's Facebook feed. In her profile picture, she is bright, smiling happy looking girl brandishing a latte. A far cry from the disheveled crying mess I see in front of me. Lina nods.

"On October twelve did you write the following post?"

The image changes to her post: *OMG. Some people need to accept certain things aren't ever going to change. I'm trying so hard to diffuse the situation but some people just want to exasperate things.*

Lina looks confused, "yes that's mine. How did you get that?"

Mrs. B shakes her head, "Do you see anything wrong with this post?"

"No, I don't." She challenged.

The image changes again, this time to the same post but with three words underlined in red; Except, Diffuse and Exasperate.

"Three improperly used words, Miss Tran. Unacceptable. It is 'Accept' not 'except' and 'Defuse' not 'Diffuse.'"

Lina looks around. That poor bitch is as confused as I am. "So what? What does it even matter?"

"It is the English language, Miss Tran, it matters a great deal." Mrs. B's eyes go wild again as she stands up in her seat, her fingers pressing the small remote that controls the projector. Slide after slide of Lina's posts and her comments on friend's posts. All butchered with manically drawn red circles. "Look at all of this, look at your flagrant disrespect for the English language. You've insulted every teacher that has ever spent five minutes with you. You've insulted every student who has opened a book or taken pen to paper. Your disregard for the basic architecture of our beautiful language is disgusting. So much ignorance, so many misused words, misspelled words, wrong connotations, wrong emphasis' placed. This," she screeches, as the slide comes to a picture of an essay written by Lina that looks like a pig had been butchered on it – so much red. "How you got any kind of passing score is a mystery that shall stand the test of time like the Nazca Lines. YOU ARE AN IDIOT, MISS. TRAN."

Lina bursts into sobs and buries her face in her hands.

"Weep for Hemmingway or for Fitzgerald, for they are who you have hurt here tonight." She sits back down. "Mr. Calvin, does the Defense have anything to add?"

The lawyer turns to Lina shrugs and shakes his head before throwing his hands up. "Defense rests your Honor."

"What?" Lina looks up at him in disbelief. "Do something," she pleads. "Don't just fucking sit there."

"Look, I'm sorry but you did this to yourself. You could have used spellcheck."

"SPELLCHECK DOESN'T WORK WHEN YOU MISUSE A WORD." Lina jumps up from the table. She points at Mrs. B, "who the fuck are you to pass judgment on me? Who?!"

"I am an English teacher Miss. Tran, the last protectors of our great language. Next only to copy editors, god knows they do their part. So yes I will pass judgment here tonight on you, and your entire heathen, illiterate generation! Like Mr. Marques who is awaiting his turn." She presses the remote again and a series of text messages appear on the screen.

I assume the Marques she speaks of is another of the bound and gagged group waiting against the wall. "Mr. Marques, your smartphone has a keyboard and autofill capabilities. There is no reason to use the archaic text message abbreviations from the early aughts. NO ONE HAS A FLIP PHONE ANYMORE YOU LAZY JACKASS."

She takes a breath and regains her composure before she bangs the gavel. "A law was put on the books back in seventy-two, and it is as relevant today as it was then. It has been amended of course to adapt to the more current issues of the times. It is the one I fall back on too often in cases like these. Lina Tran, you have been found guilty of Assholism via Social Media. You've spread Assholism like a sexually transmitted disease, infecting everyone you've interacted with. You have defiled our great and sacred language and therefore should receive the full extent of punishment that this court is authorized to dole out in the name of Geoffrey Chaucer. Bailiff."

The imposing black gentleman moves faster than I imagine he was capable of doing. He snatches Lina Tran up in a quick movement. Tucks her under his arm like carryon luggage and carries her into that little room I saw on the way in slamming the door shut behind them.

Mrs. B composes herself and the lawyer does the same. I can hear Lina Tran's screams very clearly, and for some reason, that does it for me. I am totally over this shit.

I stand up rather abruptly, so fast it even takes me by surprise. I raise my hand again, like a kid in school. Jesus, I'm lame but Mrs. B is pretty fucking intimidating.

"Yes, Delicate Homosexual."

"Look, I don't know what the fuck this is." I wave my hands around, pointing at everything in the room, "what the fuck you're doing." I turn around and point at the men in suits. "And who the fuck are these two? Seriously I really want to know who the fuck they are." I take a breath. "Ya know what, no, I don't care. I have money, and I wanna buy some weed and I want this fucking night to be over and done with. Now I have been through some shit this evening and if you want to spend your time judging people on their bad grammar, go for it. You do you Boo-boo. But I'm out, so, Mrs. B, your honor, your excellence, whatever it is you want to be called, can I buy some motherfucking drugs or what?"

She looks at me and sighs deeply. "I'm afraid I'm all out tonight, I've only got my personal right now and I don't see my connection for another week. I apologize."

Flames.

Flames on the side of my face.

The anger, oh the furious blinding anger. I can feel my face getting red. My internal body temperature rising. I go to scream, to shout, to roundhouse kick a chair across the fucking room. Instead, I take a big deep breath.

I exhale and turn calmly to DJ Joey Watts, who looks up at me with a dumb, stupid look on his stupid ass face. I could be at home. I could be on my couch, or even better in my bed. This whole night could have ended hours ago. But no, I let the dude with an asshole the size of one of those weird holes in Serbia, talk me into this bullshit. I flash him a smile before I ball up my fist and slug him square in his jaw. He falls out of his chair and lands on the cold basement floor with a harsh thud.

7: Pink Flamingos

Yeah, I may have, somewhat, sort of, overreacted back there. But, come on haven't I been through enough tonight? So what if he saved me from the dudes with no dicks, he deserved to get punched. It's not like I hit him that hard. I've punched two people in my whole life: Tommy Brandshow in the third grade. Fucker took my juice box. Ken Peterson in high school, oddly enough because he too took my juice box. So it wasn't like I hit him with the force of an MMA fighter or anything, but he did remain seemingly unconscious on the floor as I made my less than graceful exit from Mrs. B's basement.

Basically, I jump over some chairs, shoot the unaware bailiff with a tranq dart, and ran my ass off out of there. Though still better than anything Jeremy Renner did in that Bourne movie. I run through some backyards until I jump over and hide behind a hedge. I can hear the Bailiff's looking for me, their raised voices echoing through the quiet night. I inch away backward until I bump into something and fall forward in the bush. Facedown in the brush, my ass most likely up in the air, again. Yeah, this is my night. I feel a couple of sets of hands grab the waist of my jeans and pull me out. I fall out onto my back and look at three pre-teens circled around me wearing camo face paint, and with household items taped to the arms, legs, and chests like armor.

"You okay dude?" The main boy, who is wearing his catcher's outfit from his little league team with cookie sheets duck taped across his chest, introduces himself as Billy as I sit up.

"I've been better. What are you kids doing out here so late? Why are you dressed up as Lord of the Flies?"

"What's that?" A young black boy with a mixing bowl strapped on his head and knives taped around his arms like Shredder from Ninja Turtles, asks as he looks at me intently for an answer.

"It's a book. You'll read it in high school."

"Yeah, if we make it to high school," Billy adds. "We're going to kill the pedophile that lives a couple of houses down."

Say what now?

"He got me last Easter." The third boy, who was chubbier than the other two, added. "I thought those eggs were filled with candy." He lowers his head, "just Nyquil."

"He's touched our asses for the last time!" Billy shouts.

"Our asses will remain untouched!" The trio shouts together.

Well, then it appears I've stumbled onto some pre-teen vigilantes. Wonderful. "Just call the cops guys okay."

"Man cops don't do shit." Billy kicks at the ground. "We're going to deal with this *our* way."

I admire his determination.

"Mr. Hess is sneaky. He loves being a Pedo man. Loves boys' asses and he's made sure he can't get caught." The chubby one says, slapping a baseball bat into his hand repeatedly.

I reach under my shirt and pull off the small pack and hand it over to Billy, who gives me a quizzical look. "It's a tranq gun. There's one dart left. I was saving it because my night, well anyway, you guys need it more than I do. Shoot him with it and he'll be out for a few hours."

"Enough time to shove this up ass good and proper," Chubby adds gripping the bat.

"Jesus!" These tweens mean business. "Do what you gotta do fellas."

They lay on their bellies military-style and crawl through to the next yard. Billy looks back at me, gives me a nod and then presses on. Once again Derek Collins has been an accomplice to a crime. Good times. Good times.

I don't think things through. Maybe that's become apparent over the course of our evening and I must vow to change that starting tomorrow. If I ever make it to tomorrow. The bright side is I'm not getting a bat shoved up my Hershey highway like Mr. Hess.

Being lost in the city is one thing. I could hail a cab or ride the subway, there's always a way home. Hell, I could have walked if I had too. What I cannot do is walk home from the suburbs at two o'clock in the morning. I vaguely remembered the roads Joey took to get to Mrs. B and I follow them back to the main strip, and the plaza that has the Applebee's in it.

The parking lot is empty, naturally, and all the shops closed, even the big grocery store that commandeers the center of the plaza. The payphone in front of it no longer has a receiver attached. And why would it, it's fucking twenty fifteen who uses these things anymore – no fucking body that's who. Besides whom would I even call and call collect on top of that?

Wait, is that even a thing you can do anymore? Jesus, I'm old. Plus I don't have anyone's number memorized. If I had been taken hostage the poor kidnappers would give me back. I would not be able to tell them any numbers to call for a ransom. Everything is on my phone. My poor phone which I turn over and over in my hands trying to will it back to life. Its large screen dark and cracked, dead and unresponsive to my touch just like all the guys I date.

Well, Derek, you've fucked yourself real good this time.

I sit on the edge of the sidewalk and ponder my life choices. There are no gas stations, at least as far as I can see from my position. I could walk back toward the highway. There would have to be one near the on-ramp and undoubtedly it would be twenty-four-hour one at that. I could call a taxi. It'd be pricey but hell I got this weed money that is apparently never gonna get spent.

I close my eyes and throw my head back for a moment. I am so fucked. I am so hungry and tired, and I have never wanted to be home as much as I do right now.

That's when I hear a vehicle pulling up. I open my eyes and am blinded by the headlights of a beat-up blue Chevy truck. I freeze for a moment overcome with terror. I'm gonna get robbed, beat up, or killed. Yep, that's it, I am going to be killed. Maimed, with my head cut off, thrown into a dumpster. Derek Collins, the boy who likes to accomplice, found dead in a ditch. My mother would have a strange sense of entitlement if that happened.

I can see her now at the funeral. Telling everyone who comes near she always said if I wasn't careful I'd end up dead in a ditch. Now she was probably about to be proved right. As if my being dead wouldn't suck enough, she'd have the smug attitude of a woman who gets to brag how right she was. Fuck.

I hear the door of the truck slam shut. Then a very thick sounding southern accent shouts out, "Shit, I'd thought it was open all night."

I stand up and move away from the headlights. I see a fairly tall guy, roughly about my age, rugged but good looking in jeans and a dirty white tank-top.

"No, it's closed," I say, wondering why I am even talking to this country bumpkin. He'll take one look at me, call me a fag and then who knows what next. Beat the shit out of me most likely. Whatever it is I'm sure it won't end like the porno's I've seen.

"well fuuuck, hey you need some help, chief?"

Oh, straight men why is it always 'buddy' 'pal' or 'chief' with them? "You could say my night hasn't really gone the way I was expecting."

"I know the lyrics to that song my friend."

"So not to be forward or anything but any chance you have a cell phone? I need to call a cab, or an Uber to take me back to the city."

"The city? Well, hells bells man you are having you a night. Well, partner, I'm sorry but my phone is all out of minutes right now."

Really Jethro? Who the fuck even still has minutes? Did I fall back in time to two thousand five? Get a goddamn data plan.

"If ya want I drop ya somewhere that does have a phone, can't take ya back into the city though man sorry." He spits off into the distance. How charming.

"I wouldn't have asked you too but yeah anywhere you can drop me will be awesome if it's not an imposition."

"Hell ain't no impo-whatever ya said, hop in there buddy."

I move around to the opposite side of the truck and open the door. Climbing in I notice the passenger side floor is covered in dozens of empty Marlboro packs and it reeks of stale cigarette smoke.

He climbs in the driver side and shuts the door. He turns to me with his hand extended, "I'm Barry,"

"Derek," I say shaking his hand. "Thanks for this."

"No problem pal, see someone in trouble ya help 'em out."

I instantly feel bad for all the times' people needed things and I ignored them. 'I never saw your text' will probably be scrawled on my tombstone. Please, like *you* have time to help everyone you come across, judge someone else, Judy.

Barry pulls out of the parking lot and heads down the main road. I watch him as he drives. The more I study him, the hotter he becomes. Sure his hair is a greasy, unwashed mess slammed into a black hat with a Marlboro logo, obviously a gift from the company for being such a devoted consumer of their product. His skin is overly tanned, so I assume he works outside. Construction maybe? Or a farmhand. I have seen a few movies about the lives of farmhands, quality films of course.

His body is on the cusp of being scarily thin, but he isn't there yet and still has the lean swimmers build going on for him. I look at his white wife-beater and can envision the V lines at the bottom of his torso. Beckoning me like sirens to the promised land of his crotch. I call them cum gutters. The jeans are tight, but I can't get a read on the goods; it could be small or mammoth. It's always a mystery waiting to be unwrapped. Even if he pulled them down and showed me a small package, I'd still have hope. Remember from a tiny acorn comes the mighty oak.

He's got a little scruff on his face, enough to give him that full Marlboro man rugged look with a strong manly jawline, nice size nose, and intense dark eyes. He is a pure country boy, the kind I grew up with back in Florida. I put my focus on my surroundings once when he starts steering with his knee which incites a small panic attack within me. He reaches over, his eyes never leaving the road and grabs one of those Crown Royal velvet bags, but it isn't a bottle of booze he pulls out, but a small glass pipe and mini-torch.

DANGER WILL ROBINSON DANGER.

Without so much as a nod, he sparks it up and takes a huge hit of what I correctly assume is meth. What in the fresh hell have I gotten myself into now? Why does this shit keep happening to me?

Barry exhales a voluminous cloud of white smoke and his body twitches. Apparently, this is good shit. He extends the pipe and offers it to me, well at least he has manners. I politely decline. Those kinds of party nights are way behind me. I never found any joy in tweaking until the sun came up.

"Wanna tell me about your night man?" He releases his knee from autopilot duty. His arms and legs twitch some more. His head bobs back and forth. Yet his eyes remain intensely fixated on the road.

I try to focus on telling him my insane evening thus far, not focus on the swerving the truck is constantly doing. I blurt it all out, well the Cliffs-notes version anyway. While I talk he just nods and does a couple of more hits.

"You telling me they had no dicks?" He finally asks after a brief silence when I've finished the story.

I can't help but laugh. "Yeah, nothing down there at all."

"Didn't peg you for a gay."

"Oh, um, okay."

"I got no problem with it. Actually, I was on my way to the only gay bar round these parts to drop off some goods. You can tag along if you'd like. I know the one drag queen there sells. I mean if you're still interested. But Jesus man no dicks at all and removed on purpose? I don't get it." He reaches down and grabs at his crotch, adjusting it. Not trying in the least to be discrete.

And here we go, I know this routine. This can go either of two ways. One, he is a piggish vulgar male and simply doesn't care and will piss, fart, belch and adjust his junk in front of anyone, not giving a damn about it and I can respect that. Even a delicate homosexual like myself has his piggish moments. Or two; after adjusting it some more he will nonchalantly and offhandedly mention how his wife, girlfriend or even fuckbuddy doesn't suck him off as good or as much as he would like. That little nugget is usually followed by more "innocent" crotch adjusting. Almost like a bird's flash dance to attract a mate in the rain forest. The homosexual is supposed to respond with a rehearsed speech about how a guy can suck a guy better because of home-field advantage. Always throw the sports talk in there to secure their heterosexuality. The banter goes back and forth until the so-called straight man whips it out and expects the gay to jump on it like a dog on a bone. Any gay guy will tell you they've been in this position.

It's a position I'm not in the mood to be in right now, so I'm hoping like it hell it doesn't show up. I am weak-willed though, so if that redneck cock gets whipped out, I'd probably suck it.

Don't judge me.

That doesn't seem to be what is happening here though. We drive for a little bit and there is a lot of crotch adjusting, I start to think it might be crabs.

"I'm fucking hungry, you hungry man?"

"Dude, I'm so hungry I'd eat pussy right about now if it offered any kind of nourishment."

His reaction to my little quip is overdramatic. Like I had just spouted the funniest shit he's ever heard of. Eh, maybe it was, I don't think he gets out too much.

Barry doesn't tell me where we are headed but I agreed to go all the way to the drag bar with him. Ya know, fuck it, I'm out here, it's fuck all late already so why not just see where this goes. He mentions we are going to stop and get some grub first but that was a good ten minutes ago. He could probably be taking me out to the woods to steal my kidneys. Or to rape and kill me, or possibly kill me *then* rape me. Barry is probably a sexual freak once he's had enough meth. Which doesn't appear to be possible, judging by the number of times he's hit that pipe.

Take the wheel Jesus, take it!

He fidgets a lot and cannot decide on a radio station during the lulls in our conversation. Country, Rap, Oldies, Rock, Pop, even Talk. Nothing seems to catch his ear. Once he gets to the end of the dial, he goes back and starts all over.

Finally and oddly enough he stops on the Pop station. Taylor Swift is droning on about being twenty-two or some shit. He leaves it. His hands tapping on the ripped steering wheel cover rhythmically. Well, color me surprised.

"I fucking hate Taylor Swift," he finally declares after a few minutes of silently mouthing along to the song. "I like her music, it's pretty catchy. But she likes to portray herself as this wholesome girl and the fucking media eats it up. *"Oh, she can't find love."* *"Poor Tay-Tay dumped again."* Gimme a damn break. She got famous and jumped on every celebrity cock she could find. Don't get me wrong, I'm not judging her. Hell, she should get it, if she can get it, and more power to her. Any woman who owns her sexuality should be commended. But she doesn't own it, she pretends it's not there, despite the fact we all know her sordid details. Man after man."

Barry's pop star tirade goes on for what feels like forever. No one was spared from his critique. Poor Katy Perry, he was especially brutal on her. I dunno what it is she did to Barry, but damn. Boy when those meth heads get going, watch out. I, of course, think about how this animated vigor would translate to the bedroom. It makes him just a little bit more attractive now. What? I can't help it, I'm delirious from hunger and sleep-deprived.

Salvation. In the middle of all these damn woods and the few scattered industrial buildings we have passed, there is a small brightly lit convenience store. It looks completely out of place. For a moment I think it may be some art installation like Prada Marfa in Texas. There are remnants of what used to be gas pumps. The windows are caked with dirt but filled with neon signs promoting different beers. Most of them only half working at this point. If you're looking for a cool refreshing Budwe - this is your place.

I am more than a little apprehensive as I follow Barry through the double doors that are plastered with Lotto promotional art. I can't win it unless I am in it! So they tell me. Wouldn't that be a goddamn hoot, I win millions at a rundown store in Bumble Fuck County. I'd probably shout out I was a winner and they would kill me right there. Smack me over the head with some blunt object, take my ticket, and throw my body in the woods never to be found. Thus ends my story. I wonder how much meth six point four million dollars would buy Barry.

The doors close and a loud bell goes off. I snap out of my own head and look around. There's the checkout counter where my eyes meet the squinty eyes of an old woman behind the register. She glares at me for a solid minute and I think she is asleep until she snorts and shakes herself awake. Grunting as she sees us, Barry goes up to her and starts pointing at cigarette packs.

To my right are four aisles down the length of the store and along the sidewall is fountain machines and all the way in the back are the coolers. Against the wall in the front, there is a dirty, torn old leather sofa. A ginger-haired girl is laying on it, scribbling into a notebook. She is wearing a long floral printed summer dress, and there is a crown made of flowers in her hair.

She looks up at me and smiles, "anything can be a dildo if you're brave enough."

I avoid looking down between her legs, but from her arm movements I can, she is indeed going to town on herself. I shudder to think what she is using. Jumping up she starts twirling and dancing, reciting Lana Del Ray lyrics as she does. She is missing her shoes and her feet are nearly solid black with dirt. *"Been trying hard not to get in trouble, but I, I got a war in my mind."* She sings dancing over to me. I back up and put my hand out. She doesn't take the hint and gets closer. She reeks of booze and patchouli. Goddamn hippies. I move away.

Behind the counter I see an older man turning over the hotdogs on that little treadmill they're on that supposedly cooks them.

I wander a couple of the aisles, sourcing out what I would devour first. I love those Tastykake glazed apple pies so I'm hoping they have them. What I find however are things I've never heard of. If the label isn't in Japanese or Spanish, then it's an off-brand I've never seen in my life.

I was pretty poor in my twenties. I'd just moved to the city from Florida, didn't know anyone, and had a tiny apartment that didn't even have a stove. So I was a connoisseur of the off-brand product. I ate that cereal that came in bags okay. We do what we have to do in times of poverty. Those days may be far behind me, but I still know these are the off-brands of the off-brands. I've never heard of any them. I give up and walk back to the coolers. A nice jolt of caffeine would certainly spur my second wind.

Dammit, more off-off-brands, who's ever heard of CareRite Cola? Not me, fuck I'd even settle for an RC cola at this point. It'd be disappointing but I'd drink it.

Behind me, I hear moaning. I turn and see the spaced-out hippie chick. She hikes up her dress to her waist, slides off her floral printed panties and tosses them on the ground. She pulls herself up onto the counter and straddles the Icee machine, or more correctly the Sluree Machine, yeah Sluree not Slurpee. She turns on the nozzle and throws her head back. I stare on in horror as the thick cherry flavored ice drink begins to ooze out of the nozzle and down into her crotch.

I am in a level of hell Dante forgot to include in his literary works.

She struggles to maintain her position as the enjoyment rushes over her body. Watery cherry ice slush and what I can only imagine are her own vaginal secretions are collecting on the floor in a puddle.

Surely this is a health code violation. Where's the inspector when you need him? I wish I could take a video. Fuck my phone being dead. No one is going to ever believe this.

She achieves a very vocal orgasm and collapses onto the floor in the large puddle of icy grossness. The puddle is expanding and spreading, heading to the tips of my shoes. I back away.

From the opposite end of the aisle the old man comes barreling toward us, fuming. "Goddamit Ginger Lynn I've told you a goddamn dozen times to stop fucking the slush machine. The repairman ain't gonna fix it no more. Goddamn pussy juice all over the nozzle, pubes in the damn trap! Shave that pussy and stop fucking the goddamn machine. You's a stupid-"

He doesn't finish his rant. In his fervor, he doesn't realize the puddle and up and over he goes, slamming down hard on the floor. I fear for him for a moment until he angrily spits out the words. "Goddamn pussy juice," before passing out.

I instantly do what any good, rational thinking person would do...

I walk away.

I grab a diet CareRite cola and a weird bag of Japanese somethings that I believe are chips. There's no English writing on it except for a picture of a rooster and the word COCK really big over it. I can't go wrong with this, it is my favorite flavor.

I throw some money at the sleeping Asian woman and rush out to meet Barry at the truck. I breathe in the fresh air, so happy to be out of there. Barry is sucking down a cigarette leaning against the truck as I start eating the Cock chips.

They're not good.

The soda, if you can call what is basically caramel-colored water "soda", is also disgusting. Yep, I know now this is going to cause me some gastral intestinal distress.

Yay me.

Yay fucking me.

Eric David Roman

8. Eat Your Makeup

Barry and I continue on after the pit stop from hell. As predicted the off-off brand rations I scarfed down and are now engaged in civil unrest with my intestines. Barry, cute simple Barry, is oblivious to my plight. He keeps hitting his pipe and dissertating on the current state of country music. I don't know anyone he is talking about so I just imagine him driving naked. We pass a few more industrial buildings. Then, finally, he turns into a gravel parking lot.

There's one street lamp on the far side of it. With it, I can see a few cars are still scattered around the parking lot. Near the right side of the building, I see the same seventies-era brown conversion van I saw in the city and at Mrs. B's. It's too much to be a coincidence. I know instantly I should not have come with him, but it's too late now.

He tells me this quaint little gay bar is called Dockside. There's no sign to announce this to any onlooker though. Barry walks into the club with casual ease like he owns the place. There's a small alcove when you first walk in and small podium, obviously for some

ID checker to be stationed at. No one is checking anything tonight apparently. I think it's past three a.m. now which means everything should be closed.

As we pass around the alcove, I see the bar ahead of me. Same kind of bar you see in every place like this, tacky old rope lights half secured under it. Along the wall a dirty mirror behind the bar, with dusty bottles of booze lining glass shelves. They also have at least an inch worth of dust on them. There is no one behind it tending at the moment. There are however two elderly gentlemen sitting at it engrossed in their own conversation. They pay no attention to us. In front of the bar is a collection of small table and chairs. Toward the far side to my right is a small dance floor which doubles as the "stage" for the drag performers. Though right behind the dance floor is an actual small stage adorned with glittery old curtains tied back at the sides.

The flashing lights are still wildly blinking, beckoning out to anyone to come dance under them. Along the left and right side of the dance floor are chest high thin bars that run the length of the dance floor with their own stools. I assume this is where they put the closeted straight men to keep them in line.

I have a few bars I go to in the city, a couple that do amazing drag shows as well. My favorite is The Feathered Pearl. It's a small club, basically like all bars, clubs, and restaurants in the city. You're crammed as close as humanly possible to as many people as the fire marshal will allow in and you're forced to make friends with everyone and their HPV. I only go after I'm good and drunk or stoned. Fuck dealing with people when you're sober. It showcases some of the most amazing drag talents in the city, a few of whom even appeared on RuPaul's Drag Race.

There would be no quality like that here I am sure. And as soon as that very thought had finished, *she* walks up. She is a veritable nightmare in the flesh and not in that fun Halloween kind of way. She is on a decked out gold glitter iPhone, whatever that huge one is that takes up half your face. She is laughing, and it sounds like a school of dolphins being raped by sea lions.

"You know what makes Teddy Grahams taste better right? Semen!" Another school of dolphin squeaks erupts from her over-lined, horrendously colored lips. "Barry is here, I'll talk to you later." She removes the phone from her face, the screen now caked in her makeup. Shockingly though, the screen wasn't cracked. "Baaaarrryyyyy," she coos, drawing out his name. "Have you got my special treats?" She bats her Walgreens brand false eyelashes at him, one of which is half falling off.

I want to say she's had a rough night, but I think this is just her look.

Tragedy.

Barry smiles and hands her a small baggie filled with white powder. She wastes no time in scooping her glitter-adorned pinkie nail into it and shoving two bumps, one for each nostril.

Yes, I too always like to do hard drugs in front of complete strangers.

She looks up at me and smiles. Dear god, there are only two solid teeth left. They are as far apart from each other as physically possible. They look as though they are trying to escape her mouth. The rest of her "teeth" are crusted little Chiclets smeared with her Slutsicle Orange shade lipstick. She extends her hand out to me tilted down like she's a real lady or something. She introduces herself as "Maé Daeé."

I lean forward and smile. "No one is coming." My snarky little comment goes over her head as she continues to flash the horror show she calls a mouth at me.

"Barry, I am so happy you're just in time."

"Good, good," he looks around the empty bar. "So is Abortia here somewhere? Need to know if she's holding. My friend here needs some grass."

"How adorable, a pot-head." The deranged Lisa Frank experiment eyes me up and down like I'm the last piece of pie on the dessert table.

"Look, bitch, I'm hardly a pot-head. I am just an adult recreational drug user. I use within moderation and display impeccable self-control with my habit. How dare you assume I get blazed and watch *Scooby-Doo* on the couch while eating cereal." I mean, I do but this bitch doesn't have to know that. "Maé, how about you spin around on those blatant Louboutin knock offs. Go get this Abortia, and get out of my facial." I blow her a kiss.

I apologize for getting so gay, but when in Rome.

She pops her tongue at me, making that annoying sound that will eventually, one day, drive me to kill someone. It may very well be this ugly hoe right here. Yet another trial to add to the books for old Derek, this time though I'm the star.

Maé does actually spin around and waddle off, her poorly hand-sewn dress is so tight on her, I imagine underneath it looks like a pork loin hanging at the butcher shop. All segregated into sections with string. I shudder at the thought of her taking her clothes off at night.

She moves past to the right of the stage/dance area and into a door marked Private. To the right of that is a small alcove where I spot the restrooms. It feels like the civil unrest in my lower intestines has now revved up into a full-on civil war.

I will have to do the unthinkable. I may well have to boom-boom in a public space. The very thought fills me with a cold dread. My delicate homosexual ass will have to touch some filthy toilet seat just ready to infect me with who knows what. It's foolish I know. I am very well versed in sexually transmitted diseases. I know you can't catch things from toilet seats. I know that in fact, keyboards are far filthier than anything found in a bathroom. Really though after all this time together do you not realize I'm not the most rational thinker? I am okay for the moment. Plus this bar is empty, so, If I did go no one would even come in most likely so it'd be almost like boom-booming at home.

The door to backstage opens and another train wreck of a female impersonator walks out. This, Barry tells me, is Abortia Clinic. She is six foot tall, taller even with the heels on and thin as a rail. She is wearing a long gown that looks like it's from the seventies. Not like it was designed to look like it was from the seventies in that fashionable kind of way. More like it was found in a box in her dying Aunt's basement and Abortia thought "Hey this would look good!" and threw it on. Probably stole some other shit from dying Aunt's house too.

No Abortia, just no.

It is apparent that Dockside is not offering the crème de la crème of drag talent. I'm beginning to understand why this club is so far from civilization. Her face makeup is less garish than Maè's but her contouring is out of control. Her cheekbones are so high they're touching her wig line. Her nose looks so thin it's almost nonexistent. And though she has attempted to cover them with glue and foundation she cannot hide the huge caterpillars she calls eyebrows. She's had some kind of injection in her lips as they are bulging out to the point that they are overtaking her face. I cringe at the thought of her out of makeup. A blowfish with collagen,

As she approaches I can smell her dress. Oh yeah, you heard me right, I can smell the dress, and believe me it's stank.

"Hey Barry," her voice is so deep and baritone it's a bit startling. She makes absolutely no attempt to sound feminine. "You were looking for something?"

"Yeah, my friend here, I told him you may be able to help him out with some weed. He's had a rough night."

She looks at me and frowns. Well, at least I think she is frowning. She really should be using flashcards displaying the different emotions on them, so we know what is going on with her face. "Sorry baby, all-out, only have my personal. But you're welcome to hit my bowl if you'd like."

"Yes please." Fuck it. I need something if this cavalcade of nonsense isn't ever going to end. At least let the warm embrace of mother cannabis protect me.

Abortia opens her clutch and removes a small pipe. It is green like jade and carved to look like a naked lady. The top of the pipe is the amply carved breasts. The Green Lady does not have a head as that's the bowl. The body of the pipe after the breasts is the lady's torso down to her crossed legs. Her feet are not there because that's where the mouthpiece is.

"Let the Green Lady get you high." Her baritone voice instructs. I place my lips on mouthpiece, light it and inhale. This shit is strong. I hold it in for a solid minute and I can feel it the moment I let out my exhale. I greedily hit it two more times before handing The Green Lady back.

"Thank you so much," I smile at Abortia. Again her expression is undeterminable. I'm getting this bitch those flashcards for Christmas. So I assumed she smiled back at the good deed of helping a stranger in need. We'll never fucking know.

"It is good shit, should have probably told ya to take baby hits, but you look like you needed it. It will make the floor show all that much better."

"The what?"

She winks at me and saunters away, like a giraffe wearing high heels. I visualize a lion jumping out of the darkness and taking her down. I start laughing to myself.

Barry and I help ourselves behind the bar and grab a couple of beers. He takes mine from me and tilts it a certain way on the edge of the bar and with a quick movement snaps off the top. He hands it back to me and I swoon a tad bit. Maybe it's this Kush, but suddenly he's far more attractive than he ever was before. The way he smiles at me when he hands me my beer. The way he is standing so close to me, almost shoulder to shoulder. Yeah I know, a straight meth-addicted country boy. Could I be more cliché? It's all adorable in my mind, and like that, I'm seventeen all over again.

I had a crush on Jarrod Marko, this really cute straight boy from school. Somehow the universe had brought us together, two people whom you'd never expect to be friends. Especially since it was a central Floridian high school, and in the nineties no less. But there we were, hanging out all the time. He took me mudding once, a "sport" where rednecks take their big trucks to a muddy field and just spin around making a mess. It was terrifying in that truck. He hooted and hollered as the mud sprayed all over the windows. I had never been that scared, but I was with him. So I knew it'd be okay no matter what happened. That night, after the mudding ended, he invited me to stay over at his house. It was a rundown trailer on this little piece of land all by itself. It had that awful faux wood paneling on the walls you know and his Mom had a velvet picture of Elvis and lots of Nascar memorabilia. We stole beers out of the fridge and sat on the porch. He smoked cigarette after cigarette while we drank. He'd talk and I'd just watch him. All I wanted to do was proclaim my love for him and he do the same. I wanted him to be my boyfriend more than anything. That night we stayed up really late watching a VHS copy of Evil Dead on his tiny twelve-inch television. We laid next to each other on his twin size bed. So close to one and other on that tiny old mattress. He was shirtless the whole time, just kept his tight Wranglers on. I'd move my arm every once and a while like I was stretching just to feel his warm skin against mine. I relished every moment that my arm grazed his stomach, or my leg rubbed against his. Drunk, and tired, we both passed out before the movie was even over.

Unrequited love, it sucks ya know.

Do you guys think Sean Connery is doing okay? Like did he take his meds? Does he know what day of the week it is? Is he watching a Bond marathon on AMC right now and making fun of Roger Moore?

My rambling train of marijuana-induced ruminations is interrupted by yet another horrid female impersonator. This one introduces herself as Summer Clearance. She's a piece of work, a cheap Party City wig, torn pantyhose, and her makeup was put on without the aid of a mirror, in the dark, and on a train apparently. A walking disaster movie, at some moment the Rock is going to chopper in and rescue people.

Her voice is her most grating feature though. It's high pitched and she draws out every other word longer than it needs to be. If only I had a brick I'd probably commit a hate crime right fucking now. Thankfully Barry hands her an eight ball of coke and she bats her eyes at him. He waves her off with his hand while focusing his attention away from her. Bitch has tried to get him before apparently. He ain't having none of it. I want to back him up with a "hit the road sista," but I remain silent. I'm really high so I can't be sure what will happen if I speak. Nothing may come out or everything will. It's a coin toss at this point.

"The flooooooor show will start soooooooooon."
She snaps her fingers as she walks away. Somewhere
Summer's father is sobbing softly into his hands in his
study, wondering where his little boy went. I think if
you're quiet enough you can hear his heartbreaking.

The flashing lights and the music stop abruptly.
Which honestly startles me and slightly freaks me out, I
grab Barry's arm. He turns to me and starts laughing. I'm
sure my eyes are glazed over. Maybe even my pupils are
dilated and are wide open. I look like one of those Funko
Vinyl Pops come to life. I'd go look in the mirror in the
bathroom but I'm honestly too stoned to move. He
doesn't move my hand from his arm though, he just lets
me grip it.

The weed is seriously fucking with my mind. It
sounds like a concert is on in the background. I hear
music that the club isn't playing. I feel like I am outside
of myself. I am standing, clutching the arm of Barry, but
I'm beside myself seeing everything happening. It's
fucking amazing. I am so lost in my own thoughts. I do
not notice that more people have come into the club.
About six other people are milling about at the end of the
dance floor. I try to focus on them, see who they are,
what are they wearing. But, they're just blurs, fuck
maybe they're ghosts! Is this a ghost bar? Is that a thing?
I didn't think scat bars were a thing until I accidentally
went into one in Amsterdam. It was called the Litter Box
and the less said about the experience the better.

A voice cuts through the darkness, it's deep and
masculine but trying very hard to be as feminine as
possible. "Ladies, gentleman, and etcetera, it is time for
the floor show!"

The Ghosts cheer wildly as Barry puts two fingers
in his mouth and whistles loudly.

"Here she is, the one, the only...Lunestra
Sleepwell!"

The techno beat tears through the club. It's like a physical slap against my chest as I see a single spotlight shine on the center of the small stage at the back of the dance floor. Lunestra, who from this distance appears to be a radiant vision of loveliness, but I know up close she's a big old mess like the other girls in this dive.

It takes me a minute to take in her outfit. She's tall and flawlessly ebony skinned. For the most part, she's pretty fierce as she moves back and forth on the stage showing off her costume all choreographed to the music. She's clad in a loose-fitting black leather bodysuit. In random places there are metal clasps the kind that is probably from cheap belts she mopped from Goodwill. Mopped is drag slang for stolen, but you knew that. Didn't you? I'm so high. I mean I don't know if she did for sure, I'm just guessing. She doesn't seem the type to *pay* for things. Lunestra turns to her right and I can clearly see she has not, how do I say this delicately, tucked her goodies away properly. It's there and apparently begging to get out. She turns to her left and I catch a look at her as she does. I see there are two clasps directly by shoulder. Something about it strikes me as being oddly familiar.

Timed perfectly with the music she throws up her arms and reveals she's been hiding a cape this whole time. Sneaky bitch! The ghosts lose their shit at this. The outside of the cape is as black as her suit, but the inside is a dark burgundy. Again I am struck with a sense of familiarity. I do not know how long her spectacle is going on. Someone has put time on shuffle in my mind.

Summer Clearance appears off of the side and hands Lunestra a silver half mask. Lunestra takes it, lowers her head and slips it on. Her reveal to the audience is epic as the lights flash around wildly and the music begins to pump louder. The beat becomes ferocious. I stare at the silver mask, with its pointed bird-like nose, large oblong decorative eye openings, and circular design and it hits me. She's fucking dressed as Winslow Leech from DePalma's *Phantom of the Paradise*. Holy shit, she owns everything right now, she owns me. Everything I have done or been in my whole life has led to this moment and it's all for Lunestra. I scream out in my drug-fueled frenzy, "SWAN STOLE MY MUSIC AND FRAMED ME." She points at me and nods her head. She knows I get it and I get her for getting it and we both get each other in that glorious moment.

The lights begin to illuminate the dance floor where I see three other drag queens. They are sitting in the middle of the dance floor. Bound and gagged. I can see their mascara running down in dark black rivers, from eyes red and bloodshot.

Damn, I was having such a good time too.

Lunestra stands center stage, demanding every eye in the room to her. She motions with her hands and the music lowers in a volume to just a low hum. She takes a dramatic pause and looks out at me and the Ghosts. "Welcome to the floor show!" Another fling of the cape, inciting more delirium from the Ghosts, who are still all blurs. Fuck I hope they are real.

Am I real?

What the fuck is going on?

"You, my friends, are joining us here at Dockside on a rather special night. We've done floor shows before baby, but not like this!"

I take a better look at the bound group in the middle of the dance floor. I instantly recognize them as some of the queens who work at The Feathered Pearl.

"These cunts here, think they're better than us, dontcha Hunty?" She points at one of them on the floor. They protest through the yellow pee-stained jockstraps that have been stuffed into their mouths. Summer and Abortia flank Lunestra's sides. Still looking like something the cat threw up, batted around for two hours, and then dragged in. But now both are in nurse's outfits carrying metal trays. Maé emerges as well. Her nurse's outfit is three sizes too small of course, but thankfully the bottom half of her face is covered with a surgical mask. There may be a god after all. She slides two black rubber gloves onto Lunestra's hands.

"Everybody say hate!"

The Ghosts respond in an eerie chorus of voices shouting 'Hate'.

"Everybody say hate! 'Cause we hate these ratchet heffas don't we? Stupid busted hoes thinkin they run shit." Lunestra steps down onto the dance floor circling around the hostages. "Good enough for a *race* aren't they? Well, tonight these ru-diculous bitches are really gonna lip-synch for their lives."

Abortia steps down and shows off her tray to the audience. Three large gauged syringes filled with tan liquid.

"Liquid foundation!" Lunestra announces, "Not sure if we got y'all's skin tone but we'll make do."

Summer shows off her tray in the same fashion with a collection of more syringes with varying colors of liquid in them.

"Liquid eyeshadow mixed with just a hint of liquid lip liner. Only the best for our girls tonight." Lunestra moves around the bound and gagged queens giving each of them a kick and laughing wildly. "Get these ratchet cunts on their feet!"

Maé moves over and quickly gets the three on their feet. She ushers them to the stage area and positions them in a row. The three are actually really pretty, very polished and amazing looking even under the circumstances. I know two of them, Chastity Pariah and Dixie Normus.

"Now it's all very simple. See we're gonna make these bitches' insides as beautiful as their outsides and then they're gonna work the motherfucking runway for us. They're gonna work it till they die!"

The Ghosts erupt as the captured queens stare out into the audience in shock, their eyes pleading for help. I reach for my fanny pack but realize I gave it to those kids. My high is still so strong I can barely function. Barry turns his head to me and whispers how fucked up this all is in my ear. I just nod. What else can I do?

Moving like a pack of wild beasts, Summer, Abortia and Maé pounce on the bound trio. I watch in stomach-churning horror as the brightly colored syringes are jabbed into the girls' arms, into their necks, and into their faces. Summer jabs the needle under the right eye of Chastity and injects the blue liquid. She screams through the gag, as all the girls try to fight back, but it is of no use. Every time a needle is removed another one is jabbed into a different part of their body, and no way to block any of them.

I am unsure how long this actually goes on but once the final syringe of liquid foundation is emptied they back away from the girls.

"Now," Lunestra commands, sounding like an evil villain, "You better work."

The trio is unbound as Lunestra pulls a diamond handled gun out and points it at them. The music amps back up, the beat starts pounding loudly and the ghosts and I in the crowd just watch. Lunestra motions with the gun for our hostages to start.

Chastity begins first, blood and makeup oozing out of all her puncture wounds in small streams. Her face swollen in the areas the needles penetrated. She must be channeling some divine inner power because she starts off with a bang; sashaying around the dance floor with sheer ferocity as she strikes poses at every musical cue and vogues within an inch of her life. Her face is stone, not a sign of fear on it. If there were awards for 'Giving Face' she would win one tonight. As she gets closer to us at the edge of the dance floor I can see the metallic blue liquid eyeshadow beginning to seep out of the corner of her eyes. It's a more vivid, fuller blue than any blue I've ever seen. It shimmers and pulsates as it reacts to the flashing lights. She stumbles a bit but straightens herself out and resumes her routine as metallic red seeps out of her nostrils.

"Work Hunty! Work!" Lunestra screams at her in delirious satisfaction. "Let that inner beauty treatment course through you. Yaaaassss! It can't be contained! It simply cannot be contained!"

The song reaches its climax and Chastity collapses into a heap on the dancefloor. Her face frozen in horror turned outward, looking at the audience. The eyeshadow/lip liner combination is oozing out of every orifice on her face and now she resembles a painting that's melting. It's unsettling and I've seen a lot of shit tonight but this is a bit too much for me. I am delicate after and my stomach also signals me that it is unhappy.

Summer and Abortia move Chastity's body out of the way as Lunestra demands Dixie starts. As they drag her off it leaves a smeared trail of colors on the dirty club floor.

"One girl is down. Let's get the other two on the floor. We need to crown a WINNER!"

The song changes as Dixie starts dancing. Her face far more swollen than Chastity's and it looks like one eye is completely swollen shut until I realize it is just filled with green foundation.

"She's blinded by the beauty!" Lunestra cackles in delight.

Purple eyeshadow is seeping out of Dixie's ears as she stumbles and vomits up a rainbow of color before screaming for help. Lunestra moves into her and taps the gun to her temple, demanding she gets up and keeps dancing.

I let go of Barry's arm and head for the door. My stomach is demanding some attention and I can't handle anymore. I need some air. I nod when Barry asks me if I am okay and quickly and hopefully unnoticed, sneak off to the front door.

As it closes behind me, I hear the Ghosts cheer, Dixie must be down. Good lord, what did those three do to deserve that? I rush to the right once I'm outside and go around the building. The cool air makes my head rush. The earth feels like its spinning. I go past the seventies conversion van and a little bit further up into the woods. My stomach is flipping, churning and I think I'm going to throw up but then I feel it.

Feel it trying to escape from the *other* end. Oh god no, not here, not now.

Not in the woods.

Not in – god-fucking-dammit.

9: Serial Mom

You ever lie in a field and look up at the stars on a calm and pretty night?

Ever watch the stars next to a steaming mound of your own feces?

Do you like films about gladiators?

I've reached a new zenith in the low points of my life. I had explosive diarrhea in the woods. Collapsed from the sheer exhaustion of that act, and then promptly passed out high as fuck.

As I wake now I can see the sky is becoming a soft light pink color and of course I have no clue what time it is since I don't wear a watch. Why would I? I have a damn phone that tells me what time it is. I stand up, my pants around my ankles. I feel, unclean and gather up some leaves to wipe myself. And for the, who knows what time, I question how it is that I got myself here. Why didn't I just go home when Buzzington offered? Why didn't I say no to the fisting loving DJ? Why did I let a meth-addicted cutie talk me into this?

Then it dawns on me. Where the fuck is that cute meth-addled asshole anyway?

I pull up my pants, throw my shit smeared bundle of leaves down and rush out of the woods. The parking lot is empty with the exception of the van still silently parked against the side.

"GODDAMIT," I yell at the top of my lungs and kick at the gravel on the ground. "SON OF A FUCKING BITCH." I am so furious I just want to punch something. How long was I out? Why would Barry just leave me? Why am I even thinking Barry would come looking for me? I fucking met him like five minutes ago. I fight back some tears, yeah I may start crying. If I do, I'd ask that you not judge me too harshly.

I was lost once during my trip to Amsterdam, another poop-related debacle actually. I spent almost two hours searching and to find the right way back to my hotel. Eventually, I stopped in the middle of the sidewalk. Frustrated with the stupid map I had that wasn't helping I tore it to pieces in a fit. Then I started crying. I was so mad, so upset and so anxious over how I was going to get out that mess that I just lost it right there in the street.

Now I'm in a similar situation. The glow of the sun rising becomes stronger. *Well Derek, how you getting out of this one?*

"Hey, you over there," a very thick Italian accent yells at me.

I turn around and see a short woman wearing a bright pink and purple tracksuit standing next to the driver side door of the van and more importantly, I notice the keys dangling from hand. I reach into my pocket and pull out the weed money. Holding it in my fist out in front of me, I walk over to her. "Please help me get home." I plead.

"Okay, okay calm down. You queers get so excitable so easily. Clearly, you've had a rough night."

"Everyone I've met tonight is crazy and I just want to go home. Please take this money and get me as close to the city as you can."

I force my hand out again. I will not allow her to refuse me. She looks at me and takes the money.

"Look, I was going back into the city anyway. You ride with me, I'll get ya home."

Now I have a very strict policy of no hugging. I don't like hugging. I abhor it actually. But I grab her and hug the shit out of this strange round terribly dressed lady with am awful soccer mom haircut.

I release her and rush around to the passenger side door as she unlocks it and jump in. The interior matches the exterior. It's very brown, actually two different tones of brown, one a deep brown and the other a lighter shade of brown. Both ugly as shit, but I don't care. Wait, is that an eight-track player in the dash? Whatever, this is my golden chariot home.

She heaves her hefty body into the van and situates herself in the seat, as I put on my seatbelt. Last time I got into a stranger's van it all worked out pretty well.

"Look, so we ain't got no issues, I need to know you're cool." She says starting the van as she stares at me. She's not moving the vehicle until I answer apparently.

"I'm as cool as they come. I really don't care what you do or what you've done. Just get me back to the city and we're copasetic."

"Good," she pulls the van out onto the road and without missing a beat, "I kidnap people for money."

Sigh. Seriously?

It actually makes sense now. How did those people get to Mrs. B's? And the drag queens, and who knows what else. I never believed any of them just volunteered. An Uber-style business of kidnapping. Good for her.

"Like I said," I tell her, "It's all good with me. Wait, you're not kidnapping me though are you?"

"You're sitting in the front, what the fuck you think?"

Touché, I know a dumb question when I hear it. "I'm Derek."

"They call me Minivan Martha." As we drive she tells me she's divorced and the mother of three boys. I kinda hope they are those big Italian Guido types. You know with that nice hair and bulging muscles and also hope against hope that one of them is gay and single. She could fix us up and I'd get home-cooked Italian food all the time.

M.M is still going on about her family. *Who cares?* I think once I learn all the sons have girlfriends, plus I have questions about the kidnapping business. I tell her my address and a few bits and pieces of my night but not the whole thing. I can't bear to relive it all just yet. I may not even tell my friends. I'll just lie and say I went to bed early. Who is going to believe me anyway? I barely believe it and I'm living the damn thing.

We get back into the suburbs fairly quickly. Last night with Barry this trip seemed to take forever, but Minivan Martha knows her way as I imagine an effective kidnapper would need to be. I lean the seat back a little. My body aches, my head hurts, and my booty hole is still tingly from my explosive episode, really should have wiped better. The sun is getting higher and higher as we press on.

Martha answers her phone. I'm so out of it I didn't even hear it ring. I look out the window at the passing scenery trying not to listen to her conversation. Every few minutes Martha goes from a normal calm voice into an explosive, yet brief, rage-filled tirade. "He's not really doing anything this semester but working at the café, yeah, well EVERYONE KNOWS YOUR NIECE IS A WHORE TRISH!"

Out my window on the sidewalk a few feet ahead of me I spy an early morning jogger. Whenever I see someone jogging I always wish them luck in my head. I send them a silent 'good for you' and I don't really know why I do it, I just do. It's kinda contrary to the 'fuck you' attitude I exhibit most other times

"Trish I gotta, no, no, THAT'S WHAT MAKES HER A FUCKING WHORE TRISH!" Martha ends the call, throwing the phone down in the center console. She slams her foot on the gas and grips the wheel. "Look at this fucking piece of uppity jogger shit. Shoving her healthy lifestyle in my face like I'm some fat piece of shit cause what I don't fucking run? Do I get in her face when I'm eating cannoli's and make her feel like shit cause she don't eat fucking gluten!? STUPID WHORE!"

Before I even know what is happening the minivan is on the sidewalk. The impact is audible. I watch as the perky jogger in her coordinated running outfit with her tightly pulled ponytail slams against the hood of the van. She rolls up and her face smacks against the windshield. Her face is stuck in an expression of surprise as the force of the van moves her past the windshield and her body is flung to the road like a doll. I don't look back to see if she gets up. If she isn't dead, then shit, something has to be broken for sure. Either way, she isn't jogging again any time soon.

Are you fucking kidding me?

How is it that everyone single person I've met tonight is insane? It's just ridiculous by this point.

Martha turns and looks at me. "Fucking bitch shouldn't be jogging," I say sitting back in my seat like I'm going to take a nap. What? Look, I need to get home and bat shit crazy Minivan Martha is my only hope. What's one possibly crippled jogger in the bigger picture?

We press on down the road and I can finally see the skyline of the city as we turn a corner. It warms my heart. I feel like Frodo finally getting back to the shire after seventeen endings and knowing those giant eagles could have made everything easier.

I'm so close to my bed I can feel it. I will, of course, need a shower first and wash off this filthy shame. I turn my head to stretch my neck and that's when I see them out of the corner of my eye. Over on the small grassy knoll is a sunrise yoga group.

Minivan Martha stops the car. She's seen them as well and reverses the van. Slowly she begins to angle the front end at them. I hear the theme music from *Jaws* in my head. The group consists mainly of ladies and that like one random dude. Is he there for the yoga? Or is it for the ladies in yoga pants? The group situates themselves into downward facing dog.

She revs the van's engine and I tighten my seatbelt. It's not like I can't do anything. There is no stopping this crazy bitch. I grab the 'oh shit' bar above the window and brace myself.

"They think I wanna see that. They FUCKING THINK I WANNA SEE THAT! Doing their yogis in public, the sun's barely fucking up. Goddamn pretentious assholes." Flooring it, the van cuts across both lanes as it jumps the curb and barrels toward the group. She rolls down her window and shouts in a battle cry, "THERE'S GYMS FOR A REASON!"

They don't even see us coming. A few of them slam against the front of the van and ricochet off. One lady falls under and I hear the crunch of her bones. Martha spins the wheel to the right and whips the big van around to make sure it hits the ones she's missed with the first attempt. You have to appreciate her thoroughness.

There are cries of pain and screams for help from the horrified and mangled class. They're going to have a really tough time reaching Zen now with all the PTSD they're gonna have. That one random dude is holding both of his legs, trying desperately to apply pressure to his dual compound fractures. My eyes meet his and all I can do is shrug and mouth 'I'm sorry'.

"I BET YOU'LL HAVE NO PROBLEM BENDING OVER TO KISS YOUR OWN ASSHOLES NOW! NAMASTE!"

Her task done, Minivan Martha takes the van back onto the road and speeds toward the city. I see the sign for Fifty-Six. Sweet relief, I'll be back in my city and in my bed in no time.

That's when I hear the sirens.

Fuck me.

Martha speeds up and why would I expect anything different? She takes the van to top speed as we fly onto the on-ramp. Martha knows her way around, that's for sure. We're only one exit away from my exit. I can hear the sirens but can't see the police yet, but I know they're back there. I'm fucked. Derek Collins, the guy who likes to accomplice killed in a police shoot out on Interstate Fifty-Six, a fitting end to a fucked evening.

I'll be dead and have no control over the book they'll write about me. They'll quote all the wrong people, like Donna from the office. That bitch steals office supplies, who's she to judge me posthumously. They'll paint me as some sex-starved deviant fiend who spent his last night puking on dickless assholes for fun. Well, it wasn't fucking fun and I need to remain alive to make sure everyone knows that dammit.

Martha has her foot down to the floorboard so hard I think she may push right through it. She is not letting up. I can see in her face she shows no signs of going quietly. She may well kill us.

"Take your seatbelt off," Martha says turning to me.

I look at her like she's insane. We're going eighty on the freeway. I fear the van is gonna shake apart any minute.

"I'm gonna get your little delicate homosexual ass home, NOW GET THE GODDAMN SEATBELT OFF!"

I do as I am told. My exit is coming up. I still don't see the cops, but I know they're back there and so does she. She weaves in and out of the few cars that are also on the road. She yells horrendous things at them, and I learn she doesn't care for women drivers at all either, which is so odd considering what she's doing. "DO YOUR MAKEUP AT HOME AND DRIVE THE DAMN CAR YOU GASH!"

I see the hint of the flashing red lights in the side view mirror. My exit is a few hundred feet ahead. She whips that van across two lanes of traffic, horn blazing, profanity and racial slurs flying out of her mouth. We skid onto my exit and I think the van catches some air as we do, but she controls it beautifully and though the van begins to go sideways, skidding down the off-ramp, she recovers it and takes it down onto Thirty-Third Street, slowing to like forty and looks at me.

"Jump." She demands.

"Are you fucking insane?"

"Tuck and roll homo or you're coming with me and I'll BE DAMNED IF THOSE PIG COCKSUCKERS ARE TAKING ME DOWN!" She pulls a revolver from the center console. "NOT FUCKING TODAY!"

I grab the door handle. Now I've seen this done in movies, so I can do this. I'm gonna channel Linda Hamilton in Terminator Two and find my inner-

"JUST DO IT ALREADY!"

I fling the door open, take a deep breath and jump out.

10: This Filthy World

You know how in movies people dive out of moving vehicles and just get up and keep running. Yeah, so that's bullshit. I tucked and rolled and now am lying still as the grave on the sidewalk. Pretty sure my head is in some old dog urine. My entire body aches and I don't think I can even move. Luckily, it's still early as hell so the sidewalk is not filled with brunch assholes yet.

I sit up. The small of my back is sore and my right leg is throbbing. At least I'm not dead right? I summon the strength I have left, stand up and hear my back make a horrible cracking sound as I do. I envision, for a brief moment, a life of moving around by blowing in a tube. I don't care about all those reports you see about people overcoming huge physical disabilities to lead normal lives. I'd just be bitter and angry. Screw their positive attitudes. Oh you only have one leg but you ran a marathon, Fuck off.

Luckily my body is still functioning for the moment. I follow the sidewalk and realize, for the first time this whole night I know where I am. I'm only a block away from my building. I thank the goddess Madonna and start toward my building.

I catch my reflection in the window of a deli. I look like I belong in an episode of the Walking Dead. My hoodie is torn, my jeans are filthy, covered in dirty muck and who knows what else and also torn. Well, goodbye favorite jeans. The He-Man shirt is ripped at the bottom and at my collar as well. Goodbye, favorite t-shirt. My hair is a hot damn mess. There are still leaves and twigs in it from my siesta in the woods. My face is also dirty. I have a bruise on my left cheek and my right leg hurts so much, I'm limping a little bit. If this ain't a walk of shame I don't what is.

I turn the corner and see my building. My beautiful turn of the century, forty-six-floor rent-controlled building. I stop for a moment. I don't trust this. Maybe it's like when those people are stranded in a desert and they see the mirages. Maybe it's a mirage. I'm gonna get there and it will fade away. I'll still be in the woods, shooting poop fireworks out of my ass.

I reach down into my left pocket expecting to feel my keys and instead I laugh because of course, I feel nothing. My keys aren't there and then I think back and realize who knows when or where I fucking lost them. I've dove out windows, ran away from frat boys, and had my pants down around my ankles twice. My keys could be anywhere really and at this point honestly, I don't give a shit.

I wait for the light to change and I cross the street. I can hear sirens in the distance. Did Martha get away from the Popo? I hope so, she was a crazy bitch but she got me home like she said she would. Yeah, she killed a couple people along the way but hey, no one's perfect.

I approach my building and Harris, the doorman, rushes to me.

"Mr. Collins, are you okay sir?"

"I'm good Harris. I'm going to need the key to my apartment if you don't mind. I've had a bit of an evening."

"Of course sir, right away." He grabs the door and follows me in, going straight to the front desk and roots around in a drawer. After a moment he hands me my spare. I promise to tip him later and he nods understandingly. He starts to say something but I tell him whatever it is can wait to later and I waddle my way toward the elevators.

The elevator walls are all mirrored. While normally I don't notice them, today I can see all of me. So on my twelve floors long ride up. I get to the stare at the devastation a night of trying to score an eighth has done to me. "I'm a fucking walking PSA," I say to myself out loud. What can I do but laugh at the absurdity of it all?

The ding of my floor, the doors open. With the key in hand, I shamble slowly down the hallway to my apartment. I slide the key into the door and am about to turn it.

"Derek?"

The voice startles me and I grab my chest and turn to see RJ standing by the stairwell door. "RJ?"

"Yeah, I'm sorry, didn't mean to scare you."

He doesn't have any bruises or cuts on him. Apparently, he survived the frat boy death match unscathed or he's a mutant with healing abilities. Either way, he's changed his clothes and looks washed up. "What are you doing here?"

He holds out my keys. "These were in my room. I figured out which car was yours and brought it back here for you. I've been waiting for you to get back. Are you okay?"

"I'm fine. You've been waiting here all night for me?"

"Yeah, I figured you'd be back in a couple of hours after I left you." He says sheepishly, looking down at his feet like a little kid in trouble. "I kinda feel like whatever happened to you was my fault."

"It's, um, it's no one's fault. Look, I-"

"I was hoping we could hang out." He blurts out quickly interrupting me.

"I really just wanna take a shower and collapse into bed for the next week and a half."

"Oh." He looks around the hallway and then directly at me. "Can I join you?"

Excuse me? Hell to the no, I am too tired for this shit. I don't give a fuck how cute he is, how hung he is, I am not dealing with any crazier.

Before I can respond he rushes all the way up to me, mere inches from my face. "I brought you something else too, not just your car." He fishes in his pocket and pulls out a Ziploc baggie with a half of the most beautiful herb I've seen in a long time. Despite being double bagged, I can smell it and it's glorious. "I figured you would probably want this, but seems now though like you *need* it." He flashes me that smile and my already weak body weakens a little more. "Maybe we can share it if you'd want too," he says staring directly into my eyes. "Taking a shower stoned is pretty fun ya know," he leans in and whispers in my ear, "especially with another person there."

I turn the key in the lock and push the door open. I motion for him to go in.

What?

Like I'm gonna just say no?

About the Author

Eric David Roman lives with his adoring husband, his obese cat Gonk and doesn't actually like writing about himself, especially in third person – I mean its weird right? You know I wrote this. I didn't have someone do it for me. I'm not famous enough to have someone write adoring things about me. So, this whole thing is basically just me jerking off in written form for your enjoyment. Anyway, I hope you enjoyed Despicable People as much as I enjoyed writing it.